MORE THAN
A FLING?

BY
JOSS WOOD

First published in Great Britain 2014
by Mills & Boon, an imprint of Harlequin (UK) Limited,
Eton House, 18-24 Paradise Road, Richmond, Surrey, TW9 1SR

© 2014 Joss Wood

ISBN: 978 0 263 91138 1

Harlequin (UK) Limited's policy is to use papers that are natural,
renewable and recyclable products and made from wood grown in
sustainable forests. The logging and manufacturing processes conform
to the legal environmental regulations of the country of origin.

Printed and bound in Spain
by Blackprint CPI, Barcelona

Joss Wood wrote her first book at the age of eight and has never really stopped. Her passion for putting letters on a blank screen is matched only by her love of books and travelling—especially to the wild places of Southern Africa—and possibly by her hatred of ironing and making school lunches.

Fuelled by coffee, when she's not writing or being a hands-on mum Joss, with her background in business and marketing, works for a non-profit organisation to promote the local economic development and collective business interests of the area where she resides. Happily and chaotically surrounded by books, family and friends, she lives in Kwa-Zulu Natal, South Africa, with her husband, children and their many pets.

Other Modern Tempted™ titles by Joss Wood:

FLIRTING WITH THE FORBIDDEN
THE LAST GUY SHE SHOULD CALL
TOO MUCH OF A GOOD THING
IF YOU CAN'T STAND THE HEAT...

This and other titles by Joss Wood are available in eBook format from www.millsandboon.co.uk

This book is dedicated to two people
who were taken from us far too soon.

To Robbie Adam, the Third Earl of Thornham, who
lost his life spear fishing off the coast of Madagascar...
I swear we could hear your laughter whistling
through the trees at Thornham yesterday.

And to Jenny Heske—wild woman, sage, free spirit,
soul sister—who passed away in October 2013 at
the Norman Carr Cottage, Namakoma Bay, Malawi.
Smart, funny, brave and so, so wise.
Our kids adored you, as did Vaughan and I.
You will always be our Lady of the Lake.

CHAPTER ONE

'GETTING SLOW, BOSS?'

Ross Bennett slapped the ball from his opponent's hands and dropped a three-pointer into the basket. He flashed a relieved smile.

'Does that look slow?' he demanded, hands on his hips.

'Lucky,' was the quick response and Ross snorted.

It was, actually, since it was the only basket he'd landed in ten minutes. Either his geeks were getting better or he was getting old and slow; he chose to believe that they were getting better.

Despite the fact that he was getting his ass handed to him on the makeshift basketball court abutting his building by two kids just into their twenties, Ross Bennett was having a good day. It would be better if his guys were actually doing some brainstorming on the post-apocalyptic world that was integral to the new game they were designing—rebuilding the world after the apocalypse while fighting pockets of evil zombies and ghouls was not easy!—instead of having so much fun running rings around him.

'Hey, I don't mind you playing, but you've got to do some work too,' he stated as they regrouped. 'If you're not going to try and come up with ideas for our destroyed world then get your asses back to your desk.'

He saw a couple of sheepish looks and heard one 'Sorry boss...' and hid his smile. These guys were some of his best recruits and weren't sorry at all.

Ross felt his mobile vibrate in the pocket of his combat shorts and pulled it out. Lifting it up to his ear, he mouthed *zombies versus ghouls* at his staff and gestured them to carry on playing while he took his call. 'Bennett.'

'Ross, darling.'

Ross sighed at the dulcet tones of his mother. 'Hi, Mum.'

'Hi, baby.'

Thirty-three years old and he would always be her baby. Mothers. 'What's up?'

'I was wondering when you might be coming back home...back to London?'

'Is there a problem. Is Dad okay?' Since his father had had a heart attack a couple of months back it was a valid question.

'No, he's fine. Back to work.'

Back to work: such an innocuous phrase, except when used in relation to Jonas Bennett. Ross felt the familiar burn of resentment and anger.

'I was just hoping that you might come back for Hope's thirtieth birthday.'

His little sister was thirty? How had that happened? 'I hadn't really thought about it, Mum. What are you planning?'

'A family dinner.'

Since he was no longer part of the family her statement was wildly optimistic. Ross lifted his face to the spring sunlight and pushed his long, sun-streaked hair back from his face. 'Mum, I'm happy to have dinner with you and Hope any time it suits you, but I'm not ready to break bread with Dad yet.'

'Will you ever be? Will this stupid cold war ever end?'

Her guess was as good as his. It wasn't up to him. 'I don't know, Mum.'

'I hate being in the middle of you two,' Meg Bennett complained.

Then stop putting yourself into the middle, where you're going to get squashed like a bug, Ross silently told her.

'Can't you just apologise, Ross? You know how stubborn he is. Just apologise and he'll forgive you. You'll be part of the family again, he'll reinstate your position at Bennett Inc., and give you your trust fund back...'

I'd rather swallow poisonous tree frogs.

Ross dragged his hand through his hair. His father, and clearly his mother, thought that his inheritance, his trust fund and his position as the heir apparently were all-important, but he didn't give a rat's ass about any of that. His independence was far more valuable to him any day of the week.

He didn't need his father's money or approval...he just needed his freedom. He pinched the bridge of his nose between his fingers. 'Mum, I'm not discussing this anymore. I've got to go, so...'

Ross listened to her goodbyes and rested his mobile against his forehead. Then he shoved the phone into the back pocket of his shorts and tossed Table Mountain a look.

It glinted purple and green today, and was without the tablecloth cloud that was frequently draped over it. It was one hell of a view, he thought. He could look at Table Mountain from his office and the Atlantic Ocean seaboard from his house—two of the many reasons he loved Cape Town. Another reason was the fact that it was halfway down the world, so he didn't have to deal with his mother's nagging face to face. He liked Cape Town, liked the laid-back, artistic vibe, and he had no problem attracting young people to live here as it was consistently rated as one of the most beautiful cities in the world.

What was more, when he'd been trying to establish RB Media the pounds he'd saved had gone a lot further in this city than they would have done in London, and that was what had initially attracted him here.

Ross looked back towards his huge, multi-functional building and felt a flicker of pride.

RBM was *his*—achieved through blood, sweat, swearing and—although he'd never openly admit it—a couple of angry tears. Despite the fact that his father had predicted his failure, he now owned one of the most respected games and animation development studios in the world, had the most successful game on the market—Win!—and employed some of the brightest, and craziest minds in the business.

And housed on the top floor of the building was his baby: Crazy Collaborations. It funded projects—water purification, renewable energy, search and rescue detection systems—that could really make a difference in the world.

Yeah, it was all good—even if he still had to endure his mother's incessant nagging. It would be even better if his guys would stop nattering like old ladies about women— what else?—and do some work.

His geeks were suddenly silent and Ross looked around to see what had grabbed their attention this time. Silently he whistled behind his teeth.

Right, so *that* was why their tongues were dragging on the floor—and he couldn't blame them.

Light brown and gold streaky hair pulled back into a bun, sexy black nerd glasses, a knee-length black skirt that hugged surprisingly curvy hips and pulled the eyes down to the most stupendous pair of legs he'd ever seen. Those pins ended in a pair of red heels that seemed to be attached to her feet by magic. The buttons of a classic white open-neck button-down shirt hinted at the lacy bra beneath.

She looked like the hot, sexy, nerdy librarian of his teen-age fantasies, who pulled unsuspecting students behind the bookshelves to shove her tongue down their throats.

He felt a flicker in his trousers and reluctantly admitted that maybe he hadn't left that fantasy behind in his teens.

Her body rocked, but it was her face that kept his feet glued to the floor.

It was a knock-your-socks-off face—high cheekbones, made-for-sin mouth and a straight nose—a nose that was lifted high enough to give her altitude sickness.

The noise of the traffic from the road behind them faded as she approached him on those barely there, utterly ridiculous, spiked scarlet heels. Her scent reached him first: a light, citrus, grassy scent that made him think of sunshine and light. Those eyes behind her glasses—real? Fake? Who cared?—were a deep, deep blue. Both guarded and, he thought, irritated. And on closer inspection a little shadowed and baggy... Hot Librarian looked as if she needed a couple of nights of getting a solid eight.

'Ross Bennett?'

He tipped his head in acknowledgement. 'Who wants to know?'

'Alyssa—Ally—Jones. You're a hard man to get hold of, Mr Bennett.'

Good grief, *Mr* Bennett? That catapulted him straight back to Bennett Inc. and yanked bile up into the back of his throat.

'I've sent you no less than three e-mails and left countless requests on your mobile and answering machine for you to call me back. Don't you have a personal assistant?'

Ross frowned. 'Where are you from?'

'Bellechier.'

Right—the clothing and accessories company. Swiss-based, very upmarket. He recalled the messages, the requests for a meeting to talk about branding and franchise opportunities. He wasn't interested. Bigger and better brands had approached him and he'd refused them all, but he had to admit it was amusing to see exceptionally well-dressed corporate drones jump through hoops to impress him.

Ross watched as her eyes slowly swept his body, taking in his red V-neck T-shirt, cargo shorts and battered trainers. Just to see her reaction, he dipped his hand into the pocket of his pants, pulled out the band he kept there and tied the top section of his hair off his face.

Judging by the slight lift of her nose, Ms Prissy liked short, back and sides... She folded her arms across her chest and tipped her head like an inquisitive bird.

Suddenly he felt like a piece of prime rib being judged for

its freshness. If that interest was sexual he wouldn't mind so much, but her intelligent eyes were all business.

'Shorter hair would suit you better,' she said after a long pause. 'But long hair works with the bad-boy CEO vibe you have going. I'm glad you lost the goatee, though.'

Ross wanted to look around to make sure that she was still talking about him. *Bad-boy CEO?* Seriously? Surely a bold geometric tattoo on his right forearm and long hair didn't make him bad-ass these days? In the nineteen-fifties, maybe.

As for the scruff she'd called a goatee—he hadn't had one for over a year. And this conversation was starting to get weird...

'Uh...'

He caught the snort of one of his employees and without dropping his eyes from her face, he told them all to get back to their desks. When he could no longer hear their footsteps, Alyssa—Ally—pulled her bottom lip between her thumb and fingers. It made no sense that he wanted his lips where her fingers were, doing what her fingers were doing... What the hell?

Was it five degrees hotter out here than it had been ten minutes ago?

'You might just do...' Ally murmured.

Boy Wonder in his pants perked up and looked around. *Who's doing what to who? Can I join in?* Hell, he was an embarrassment to suave single guys the world over.

He scrubbed his hands over his face. 'Do you always talk in riddles?'

She flashed a row of small, white, even teeth and two shallow dimples appeared, one on each side of her mouth. He'd always been a sucker for dimples...

'Sorry... So, can we chat? Or can we make a time to chat if now doesn't work for you?'

Okay, persistent and gorgeous. *Ack.*

'Look, I don't mean to be rude...' But he would be if he had to. 'If I didn't respond to your sixty e-mails and ten thousand phone calls, don't you think that's a solid clue that I'm not interested?'

'I don't hear "no" so well.'

That, he thought, was a solid gold truth. Actually, he instinctively knew that she didn't hear 'no' at all. And here *he* was—someone who never did anything he didn't want to do and never, ever followed the herd.

A saying popped into his head: irresistible force meets immovable object.

'How did you get my personal mobile and e-mail address, by the way?'

Slim shoulders lifted and fell. 'I know people who know people,' she said mysteriously.

He wondered if he would ever get a straight answer out of her.

Anyway, as fun as it was, trading barbs with this gorgeous, ultra-feminine woman—she was a girly girl from her perfect make-up and tousled hair to her dainty toes—he had things to do. 'Got to get back to work. Enjoy your trip back to wherever you came from.'

'Geneva—and you haven't heard my proposal yet.'

'Nor do I intend to. The Bellechier brand is old-school—slick and snobby. It's everything that Win! is not.'

She had the temerity to look insulted. 'Excuse me?'

All five and a half feet of her—in heels—vibrated with indignation.

'Bellechier is one of the most iconic clothing and accessories brands in the world... I'm *wearing* Bellechier!'

Ross deliberately yawned.

'It's sophisticated!' Ally protested.

'Dull,' Ross countered, just to be argumentative. Okay, not the shoes, but everything else was. He was really enjoying the sparkle in those fire-blue eyes, the flush on her prominent cheekbones, watching her fight to keep her irritation under control. *Damn*, she was hot.

'Why would you even consider linking Bellechier with Win!? They have nothing in common.'

'They do! Of course they do—or else I wouldn't have travelled twelve hours to see you.'

He tipped his head enquiringly. 'Are you on crack?'

'Hey! I'm not the one playing basketball at—' she snapped a look at her watch '—twelve fifteen on a Wednesday morning in this heat! That's insane!'

'I suspect that my playing basketball when I should be working is what most offends your corporate sensibilities.'

He hadn't thought that nose could be lifted any higher but she managed it.

'I don't care how you spend your time, or whether you give yourself heatstroke. I just want an opportunity to talk to you about a campaign.'

Ally looked away and he sensed that she was trying to keep her cool. When she looked at him again her face was devoid of expression but her eyes were still spitting spiders.

'This isn't the way I envisaged this conversation going… I don't normally end up in arguments with potential ambassadors in the first five minutes of meeting them.'

'You do it so well,' Ross said, his voice super-bland. Time to stop baiting her, he thought. Jamming his hands into his pockets of his cargo shorts, he rocked on his heels. 'Let's get this over with, Ms Jones. Even if I was interested in exploring branding opportunities, I don't see any obvious link between Win! and Bellechier. So—not interested.'

Ally chewed the inside of her cheek. 'That's not what my brother Luc thinks. He sends his regards, by the way.'

Luc? Did he know a Luc? A memory of meeting someone called Luc at his old school friend James Moreau's thirtieth birthday party drifted into his head. And later at James' sister Morgan's wedding…

'Luc? Tall, dark, partial to smokin' hot blondes?'

Ally nodded. 'That's the one. Luc Bellechier-Smith— CEO, my boss and foster brother.'

Huh. He'd instinctively liked Luc—liked the Frenchman's passion and sense of humour, his quick mind. He couldn't imagine how and why he'd ended up having Miss Carrot-Up-Her-Bum for a sister—fostered or not.

'What do you for the company?'

'Brand and Image Director. Marketing and PR all falls under me.'

'And it was *his* idea to approach me?' he asked, now puzzled. He'd thought that Luc was smarter than that.

'Yes. We're talking at cross-purposes due to the fact that we got distracted,' she said, implying that the distraction was all his fault. 'We're launching a new line...would you give me five minutes to explain? Properly?' Ally looked at the building behind him. 'Preferably inside, where I presume it's cooler?'

'Here is good.' He was far too attracted to her as it was, and he really didn't want to extend this torture session any longer. What was wrong with him? He knew women— knew how to deal with them, how to control his reaction to them. They *never* made him feel off balance, slightly crazy.

'A boardroom would be better,' Ally countered.

His eyes narrowed in warning and he knew that she'd caught the hint when she wrinkled her nose.

'Okay, here it is, then. Never mind that my nose is going to burn and I'm going to freckle...'

He looked for freckles and could find the hint of them under her make-up. On her nose, across her cheeks.

'Bellechier is launching a new line—' Ally's opening gambit was drowned out by a piercing whistle from a balcony on the second storey of RBM.

Ross excused himself and walked quickly towards the building. Eli, his friend and number two, stood gripping the balcony railing, an anxious look on his face.

'What's the problem?'

'Jac-tech have picked up a bug in that app we sent them to test and they are not happy. You need to smooth some ruffled feathers, pronto,' Eli told him, waving his hands in the air.

Along with computer games, RBM also designed game

apps for smartphones. It was a very lucrative part of their business.

'It's a brand new app…we told them it would have bugs.' Ross slammed his hands on his hips. 'Who has their panties in a wad? The suits or the tech?'

'Suits,' Eli replied. 'Who else?'

Ross yanked the band from his hair and raked his hand through it. 'Figures. Why can't they keep their noses out of it?'

'Because they are power-hungry control freaks?' Eli threw his words back at him. 'Get your ass up here and deal with it. I'm in development, you deal with the suits.'

'Yeah, coming.'

Eli jerked his head. 'Who's the babe?'

Ross grinned and dropped his voice. 'Another co-branding offer. Give me two minutes and tell Grace to video conference Paul at Jac-tech.'

Eli saluted and turned away. Conscious of the dull headache brewing behind his eyes, Ross spun around and walked back to the source of the pain in his butt. 'I have to go.'

'But—'

He should just tell her to get lost, that he wasn't interested in any branding deals, but there was something about her—apart from her space-high hot factor—that intrigued him. It was those eyes, he realised, the layers and layers of blue. Confidence, sassiness, intelligence, and once or twice a flash of something deeper, darker. Wilder…

He knew he shouldn't, but he did it anyway. 'Where are you staying?' he asked.

'The Riebeek.'

Of course she was. Stately, old, rich… His mouth twitched. It suited the boring clothes and the severe hair, but not the shoes. Those shoes intrigued the hell out of him. 'Be in the lobby bar at seven-thirty. You can buy me a drink and have your five minutes.'

'At least thirty minutes if I'm buying,' Ally stated, in a don't-mess-with-me voice.

'Fifteen.' Ross countered, backing away.

'Twenty.'

'Twenty minutes, two drinks.' Ross whirled around and walked away. At the door, he glanced over his shoulder and sent her a wicked grin. 'Kick-ass shoes, by the way.'

'They're from the new line—the one we want you to endorse. It's not boring or snooty!' Ally shouted at his back.

Ross had to smile.

He liked women who could think on their feet. And women with dimples.

Sitting at the long dark bar in the hotel that evening, Ally felt out of her depth—and she knew that it was all Ross Bennett's fault.

She crossed one leg over the other and stared at her glass of icy white wine. She'd completely cocked up their first meeting and that *never* happened to her... She was always professional, calm and collected. She just hadn't expected the CEO of RBM to be playing basketball at noon and looking so...

Incredible? Amazing? So super-freaking-perfect that her heart had tripped over itself and bounced off the inside of her ribcage? Ally bit the inside of her lip. Within ten seconds of seeing him she'd known that Ross Bennett had the elusive X-factor she needed for the face of the new line. In fact he had it in spades—along with the sexy-factor and the hot-factor and any other damn factor she needed. That meant that Luc and Patric—the know-it-alls—had, essentially, done her job for her.

Ross would be abso-freaking-lutely perfect as the new face of Bellechier. If she, social hermit that she was, was conjuring up fantasies of ripping his clothes off with her teeth and getting him naked and on top of her as soon as humanly possible, then normal women—and not a few men—would do the same when they saw the commercials. At the very least it would make them buy Bellechier...

Lots and lots of Bellechier products. Holy smoke. The

couple of random pictures she'd found on the net had not done justice to the sheer presence of the guy. He practically radiated charisma and testosterone and heat and sexiness, and that meant…dammit…that meant Luc and Patric were right.

Blergh.

Ally glanced at her watch, realised that she still had a while to wait for Ross and returned to the primary source of her aggravation—specifically her brothers. Ally wrinkled her nose, as always uncomfortable with the word. She wasn't technically their sister—because the Bellechier-Smith family had never formally adopted her—but she had been part of their family since she was fifteen years old so what else could she call them? Anyway, they were the reason she was in Cape Town, and she was not amused because she now had to eat her words.

She hated it when that happened.

She adored Luc and Patric, and she knew that they were fond of her, but they weren't close. When she'd arrived at Bellechier Estate as their foster sister they'd both been at university and living their own lives. To their credit, they had initially tried to connect with her but she'd been distant and wary and had resisted their easily offered comfort and compassion.

Because pushing people away and stuffing her emotions down rather than expressing them was what she had been taught to do. Her father's motto had always been: *Buck up, don't cry, deal with it.* That was just what he'd done when her mother had dumped on him the six-month-old daughter he'd never known about, and she supposed that was the way he'd dealt with life. How well he had taught her to do the same.

After losing her dad at fifteen, it had been easier, and far less scary, to withdraw into the bubble of self-sufficiency and emotional independence she'd created while living with her introverted, just-deal-with-it father. Thirteen years later and that bubble now had the thickness of a Sherman tank.

She'd had some therapy, and had attended sessions long

enough to learn that she was 'emotionally unavailable'—that her father's insistence that emotions were wrong had, in the therapist's words, 'mucked her up' for life. He had tolerated her only if she was reasonable and unemotional and, despite her foster parents' encouragement to express and display her emotions, she'd never quite got the hang of it.

Emotions were messy and ugly. Indulging in them, allowing them to be a factor in her life, was like climbing into a small car the size of a sardine can and playing chicken with a F-17 fighter jet. Something was going to crash and burn and it wouldn't be the fighter jet. No, it was far better to be sensible and safe.

Why was she even thinking about her past? Ally wondered, switching her thoughts back to the task on hand. She was good at that, she thought with a twist to her lips. She could always focus on work…it was the best way to distract herself from the memories and to keep her from thinking how empty her life was. Work was where she found silent companionship, where she felt safe, needed and valued. It was a harmless place to invest time and emotions.

So, Ross Bennett… He wasn't a celebrity, an actor, a musician or a sportsperson. He was—she glanced at the folder on the seat next to her—an entrepreneur and the creator of a computer game. A computer game that was selling squijillions, apparently.

Ally recalled the conversation at a family dinner a couple of nights ago that had led to her leaving Geneva and heading south.

'Run it by me again, Luc.'

Luc had tapped the stem of his glass with his finger. 'Today's heroes are not always sportsmen or actors or models. There are others who are doing amazing things…explorers, eco-warriors, conservationists.'

'Titans, pioneers, visionaries…' Patric added, leaning forward and placing his arms on the table. 'Social media has changed the way we live our lives.'

'Computers, gaming, technology.' Luc snapped his fingers. 'Entertainment, but not films or music.' Luc's face broke out into a smile as he snapped his fingers. 'That's it… That's who I want.'

Oh, good grief, Ally thought, *this is going to come out from left of field—far, far left.* 'Who?'

'Ross Bennett.' Patric leaned back in his chair and Luc raised his hand to high-five his brother. 'Well, him and his game.'

'Win!?' Patric asked.

'Win!' Luc confirmed.

Patric whistled. 'That's pure genius.'

Win what? Ally wondered, seeing Luc's satisfied smile. She exchanged a confused look with Gina, Patric's wife. 'Who?'

'Ross Bennett,' Luc said, as if she hadn't heard the first time. 'Win!'

'Win what?' Ally demanded, frustrated. 'Stop talking in code!'

'Ross is an ex-London-based entrepreneur who relocated to Cape Town. He is responsible for bringing some of the brightest computer geeks in the world together to create the best-selling computer game…*ever.* It's a sports and leisure game called Win! He's recently been named one of the most influential people in the world under thirty-five. He is also the founder of… Jeez, I can't remember its name. but it's some kind of technology think-tank that takes the brightest of the bunch—inventors, visionaries—and lets them work on developing new tech and systems to benefit developing countries.'

Blah, blah, Ally thought, scrabbling in her bag for her smartphone. 'Yeah, but is he hot?' She caught the dual rolling of eyes and prayed for patience. 'He's selling one of the most iconic brands in the world, hot is the minimum I require!'

'He's tall.' Luc offered.

God save her from cretins, Ally thought, pulling up her search engine and typing his name in. Twenty seconds later her small screen was filled with a masculine, angular face dominated by a long nose and a rather gorgeous pair of hazel eyes. The goatee would have to go, and the highlights in his brown hair would need to be redone or taken out altogether. He wasn't, looks-wise, in the league of their other ambassadors—although she was, admittedly, making that call on the basis of a couple of grainy photos on a very small screen.

But still…on a scale of one to ten he clocked in at seven, eight… She needed at the very least a twelve.

'Jeez, Luc, I really don't think so.' Ally thought that they needed to play it safe, stick to what was trusted and true. 'He just isn't popping for me.'

Yeah, he was cute—but cute didn't sell high-end merchandise. 'Look, if you want someone different, who's related to sports, then I'll have another list of suitable candidates by morning. Suave, debonair, sophisticated candidates who match the brand.'

'I don't want someone who matches the brand. I want someone who brings a little extra. My gut instinct tells me that this is the guy,' Luc stated, his voice taking on that tone that suggested that he was digging his feet in. 'He's a new breed of CEO—part bad-ass—'

Patric leaned across the table to interrupt him. 'Did you hear about how he walked into a meeting with the boss of the biggest movie studio in Hollywood and then refused to give them the rights to adapt Win! into a movie because they were too—as he later explained— "up their own ass corporate"?'

'I read that he's sold the rights to an independent, small company because they understand the vision of Win!. He's very determined, very focused, and he marches to the beat of his own drum.'

Direct translation, Ally thought, *prima donna*. Just what she needed.

'Luc, trust me on this. He's not the right guy,' Ally said

in her most rational voice. She didn't work well with people who coloured outside the lines. They confused her.

'No, Alyssa, trust me,' Luc responded. 'I've met him a couple of times and I thinks he's exactly who we are looking for. He's rich and successful in his own right, even though he comes from a wealthy family. He's in touch with a new generation of tech-savvy people who have money. He's char-ismatic and interesting. I want you to go to Cape Town, meet the guy, and if you still think he's the wrong choice then we'll talk again.'

The wrong choice? Ally now thought. *Hah!* The per-fect choice.

Her mobile rang and she glanced down at the name that flashed on the screen. Luc…of course. She slid her finger across the screen and answered the call.

'Where are you?'

'Waiting to meet Ross Bennett again,' Ally replied in a resigned voice. 'He's a strong candidate.'

'I am the *man*!' Luc crowed with a loud, undignified whoop. Ally hoped that he was alone in his office and that nobody could hear his self-congratulations. 'And *that* is why they pay me the big bucks, ladies and gentlemen!'

'Yeah, Luc…. You *are* the man,' Ally grumbled. 'Luc one, Ally zero.'

Luc was silent for a minute before he spoke again. 'Ally, you can't possibly be upset because I had an idea that panned out…can you?'

'Maybe a little,' she admitted.

Luc's chuckle was warm and affectionate in her ear. 'You are such a pork chop, kid. We run Bellechier as a team effort—you know this. I might be the CEO but I frequently ask my dad for help and advice. When Patric gets stuck on a design he calls our mother and they talk it through. You can't find the face and we're trying to help you out. When are you going to stop taking everything so person-ally, sweetheart?'

But it *was* personal. Because if she wasn't performing

at a hundred per cent she was failing them, wasn't she? They'd given her so much, and since she couldn't give them what they most wanted—her thoughts and feelings—she gave them what she could—her labour and her loyalty. 'I'm sorry.'

'Don't apologise…you've done nothing wrong!'

His words were kind but Ally could imagine Luc shoving his hand into his coal-black hair in frustration. She frequently frustrated her very emotionally expressive and intelligent family. Dammit.

She looked for an excuse to end this conversation. 'I'm just a bit tired, Luc.'

'Tired, thin…probably undernourished. You're working far too hard and you are going to burn out, Alyssa. And then Maman is going to kill me!'

Back to this old chestnut… She'd always been thin—that was nothing new. And, yes, she was working hard, but she always had. 'Luc, I'm fine! How many times do I have to say it?'

'We don't believe you…mostly because you look like a panda and you barely touched your food the other night. Are you coping at work?'

Ally's eyes narrowed as the barman topped up her wine and she sent him a grateful smile. 'Do you have any complaints?'

'No, of course I don't.'

'Then I'm coping at work.'

Ally heard the long breath he expelled. 'You are the reason I don't have a girlfriend, Ally; I spend too much emotional energy worrying about you.'

Ally had to smile at that. 'Rubbish. You don't have a girlfriend because you have a low boredom threshold.'

'That too. Listen, with Ross try your best, okay? Be charming…funny…because despite the fact that you are as prickly as a hedgehog I know you can be both. *Je t'adore,* Alyssa.'

She wished she could give him those words back but, as always, they stuck in her throat.

'Bye, Luc.'

Luc disconnected and Ally dropped her phone into her bag. Her brothers: good-looking, smart, kind. Even if she was prepared to get involved with a man, *could* get involved, she'd probably still be single because they'd set the bar extremely high.

One day maybe she'd feel brave enough to try to find a man who matched up. Maybe one day she'd have the time to try. One day.

But not any time soon.

CHAPTER TWO

'SOMETHING WRONG WITH your wine?'

Ally looked up into those amazing green-brown-gold eyes and her heart kerplopped in her chest again. His caramel-brown hair was squeaky clean and had been left to curl down his strong neck. Even in the low light of the bar she could see the sun-kissed blond streaks and tips. Too natural to have come out of a salon, she decided, and he didn't seem to be the type to fuss. He'd removed the two-day-old shadow off his face—sadly, in her opinion—and his cargo pants and vivid red tee had been replaced with a very nice fitted pair of dark jeans and a loose button-down black linen shirt, the cuffs of which he'd rolled up his tanned arms.

Oh, yeah…he *so* had the X-factor and the Y-factor…and the make-her-hum-factor.

'Ally?'

The way he said her name, in his deep, quizzical voice, had her pulling herself together. 'Wine… Hi… The wine is fine. Why do you ask?'

'You were scowling into it.' Ross slid onto the stool next to her and ordered a beer from the bartender. Then he turned back to her and made a big point of inspecting her from top to toe. 'You surprise me, Jones. I was expecting another black and white combo. Nice.'

So he'd noticed…good. Changing his perception about Bellechier—that it was snooty and snobby—was her first goal, and that was why she'd deliberately chosen a very dif-

ferent outfit for this evening. He needed to see that their
new line was fun and casual and would suit his obviously
casual approach to life and work.

So as part of her strategy for the evening she wore the
only dress she had brought with her: a short, flouncy co-
balt number that was trimmed in black and cinched in at the
waist with a funky silver belt. It also happened to come from
the new line they were launching in a few months' time.

This morning she'd wanted to look professional, and had
opted for one of her many easy to wear, smart but comfortable outfits that travelled well. But tonight Ross Bennett
needed to get a sense of the line, an idea of what they wanted
him to promote, so she'd slipped on the dress and teamed
it with another pair of kick-butt shoes. She'd just forgotten
how damn short it was.

Now she resisted the urge to pull the skirt towards her
knees. She was not comfortable in anything that only hit
midthigh and felt particularly conscious of the amount of
time Ross was spending looking at her legs.

It made her feel squirmy and hot, unsettled. Dammit,
she wanted him to think about the line, about business,
not her legs.

Ally flushed under his scrutiny. 'Thank you. This dress
is from the new line we'd like you to endorse.'

'Okay, not what I expected.' Ross smiled his thanks as
his beer was placed in front of him. 'And that's a damn
nice watch you're wearing—very unusual. Is it also part
of the line?

'No.' Ally looked down at the man's watch that dan-
gled on her wrist. Flipping it around, she touched the face
with its very distinctive dial and ran her finger around the
oyster-style band. 'It was my dad's—the first Bellechier
watch he owned. He bought it before he even started working for Bellechier.'

'Your real dad or foster dad?'

From a flyaway comment of hers he'd remembered that
she was fostered. That was impressive, she thought. 'My

real dad. He was CFO of Bellechier for ten years and Justin Smith's best friend.'

Ross frowned. 'Justin Smith? Don't know him. How does *he* fit into the picture?'

Ally sipped her wine before she explained. 'Quick Bellechier history lesson: Sabine Bellechier is my foster mum and her great-grandfather established Bellechier watches in the early twentieth century. Sabine was an only child and she inherited Bellechier. She fell in love with the Bellechier Sales Director—Justin Smith. Justin then took over the CEO position and together they expanded into apparel and accessories. Their sons, Luc and Patric, have a double-barrelled surname: Bellechier-Smith.'

'Ah, okay. I get it.' Ross nodded at her wrist. 'So how did your dad die? And when?'

Ally's mouth dropped open. 'God, you are so nosy!'

'Then tell me to butt out.'

'Butt out,' Ally shot back, but she couldn't help but like his straightforward attitude. After the fake politeness she endured day after day it was refreshing.

She leaned back in her chair and played with her belt buckle. The words were out of her mouth before she could haul them back.

'He died of a heart attack when I was fifteen.'

In a foreign country halfway across the world. But Ross didn't need to know that—and, besides, she never spoke about those dark weeks after his death. To anyone.

'My mother left when I was a baby.'

'That sucks,' Ross said with no hint of morbidity, which she appreciated. After a little silence he sent her a mischievous look. 'You can ask me about my family if you want to. I might not answer, but you can ask.'

'Thank you, but I'm not nosy. And I'd really prefer it if we kept this conversation to the business at hand.' Mostly because she wanted to ask him a whole bunch of personal questions…which was very, *very* out of character for her. She'd learnt a long time ago about the notion of quid pro quo.

Ross slapped his hand on his chest. 'Ouch. *Touché.*' He rested his elbow on the bar and pushed his hair out of his eyes. 'So, no personal stuff. Damn, that's boring. Are we going to talk about clothes now?'

'No, the campaign.'

'Ugh,' Ross replied, taking a long swallow of his beer. 'Let's go back to talking about your clothes, then. Specifically these shoes of yours. How the hell do you keep them on your feet?'

'You're beginning to sound like you're slightly obsessed with my clothes,' Ally said, and made the mistake of slamming her eyes up to his. Green deepened to gold as she watched them heat and she could almost hear his words... *I'm obsessed with getting you out of them.*

Oh, wait—maybe that was her silently saying, yelling, panting that phrase. But there was definitely heat in his gaze...something she was pretty sure she hadn't imagined.

Ross just looked at her as she fumbled around for something to say. She was so out of practice with this man-woman attraction thing, Lord, she hadn't even been on a proper date since who could remember when.

Blow her down with a feather... And that made her imagine Ross drifting a feather over her torso, lower, lower, and following its path with his wicked mouth.

Feeling herself starting to ignite from the inside out, she fumbled for her wine glass, lifted it up to her lips and allowed the icy liquid to slip down her throat. She drained the glass and gestured to the bartender for a refill.

'I would pay a lot of money to be on the road trip *you* just went on,' Ross drawled in a husky voice...a bedroom voice.

'Uh, yeah...sorry about that.' Ally shook her head and held up her hand. 'Would you excuse me for a minute? I need to...take a...Ladies'.'

Ross stood up as she did and somewhere, in a part of her brain that still had some sort of cognitive thinking, she appreciated his manners. Pulling her bag over her shoulder, she quickly walked over to the Ladies' restroom, slammed the door open and paced the small area in front of the basins.

She wanted him in the worst take-me-now, stop-this-throbbing way. Every pore on her skin was prickling, and she was intensely aware of every breath he took, each flick of his eyelids, every movement of his strong thighs, each bob of his throat. His deep voice sneaked into places that had been so cold for so long and set her nerve-endings on fire...

She wanted to ask him up to her room for a one-night stand and the thought terrified and shocked her. They hadn't even discussed the launch of the new line, but at this moment it didn't matter and she so didn't care.

Ally shoved her hands into her hair and pulled. She'd never not cared. Who was this stranger in her head?

Ally looked at herself in the mirror above the sink and didn't recognise the flushed, wild-eyed woman looking back at her. Lifting her finger to her lips, she closed her eyes in horror. This crazy, sexy-looking woman wasn't her. She looked out of control and fairly unhinged.

Ally ran the tap and flicked some cold water onto her cheeks, patting them dry with a paper towel, taking long deep breaths to get her heart-rate to slow down. She didn't do crazy and she didn't do unhinged and she didn't put herself into situations that could get complicated...

And she never mixed business with pleasure. *Ever.* Or she wouldn't if she allowed herself to have a social life.

She'd never felt so attracted to a man. He set her libido alight with his masculinity and his hottie factor, and she could dismiss that a lot more easily if she wasn't so mentally attracted to him. She liked the fact that he was an alpha male—smart, decisive, mentally strong. He was a lot like her brothers and it annoyed her—scared her, kicked her off-balance—to realise that he would be the type of man she'd look for in the future, if or when she got her act together.

Well, this wasn't the right time, and she wasn't ready for a relationship.

But Ross isn't about a relationship, her lady bits protested. *He is pure lust...biology at its most basic form. He would be about pleasure and relief and hot, raw sex...we could do with a whole bunch of that!*

Ally gripped the edges of a basin and dropped her head. Even if she threw every caution she had to the wind—and she had a truckload—she might still have to work with him. Because, despite his current opinion, Win! *was* a perfect match to their new line, and it was her job to convince him of that. She was good at her job and she rarely failed. So when Ross became the new face of Bellechier it would be rather awkward to work with him and keep a 'pretend you haven't licked me from top to toe' expression on her face.

Because she just knew that he *would* lick her from top to toe. And back up again...lingering in certain places... Ally squirmed against her damp panties and scrunched up her face. Damp panties...? This man was more lethal than she'd thought.

Get a freaking grip, Jones! She was not going to 'do' Ross in any shape or form. That was just crazy and it was time she pulled herself together. She'd wobbled a little bit, had a strange physical reaction to him, but now it was time to be sensible and...professional, dammit. Cool. Controlled.

All the things she was so good at.

Ally put her hand against her sternum and breathed. Long, deep and slow. It was no substitute for hot, sweaty sex but it did bring her colour down and whip her thoughts into line.

If only it would work for the 'do me now' look in her eyes...

Ross placed his forearms on the bar and looked at his foot, resting on the gold rail of Ally's chair. What was he doing? He should be heading home. He still had hours of work ahead of him tonight. He had a full day tomorrow and he was nuts even to consider prolonging this evening with a rather lost beauty with dark rings under her eyes.

He'd toss back his drink, pick up takeout on the way home, take a cold shower and head into his home office.

Those resolutions flew out of the room as he watched Ally walk back towards him. She wore her hair down tonight and it was longer than he'd expected, way past her shoulder blades and naturally wavy. She'd reapplied lipstick in the bathroom and her bland corporate face was back—which was totally at odds with that sexy, sexy dress. Pity... He rather liked the flashes of wildness he occasionally glimpsed in those black-ringed navy blue eyes.

She hadn't noticed that he was watching her as she stopped between two empty tables and twisted her neck. Ross swallowed as she gripped her hands behind her back and pushed her chest out and... Hell, she wasn't as scrawny as he'd first thought. Her dress outlined her breasts and pulled across her flat stomach, lifting the hem of that dress up another inch.

In any other woman that stretch would have had him walking out through the door, because it was such an obvious move, but he could see from Ally's painfully scrunched face that she wasn't even remotely concerned whether he was watching or not. He could see pain flicker across her face as her shoulders rose and then slumped, the way her eyes contracted when she rolled her head on her shoulders.

Then she glanced across to the bar, saw that he was watching and immediately straightened her spine, giving him a long, cool look. So, Ms Priss didn't like anyone seeing her less than cool and controlled.

'Problem?' he asked when she slid back into her seat.

'A muscle in my shoulder is on fire,' Ally replied, wincing. 'I swung my suitcase off the luggage conveyor and felt the twinge. Crazy, since I'm always picking up luggage.'

I can massage it for you. Ross opened his mouth to say the words and closed it again. *And after I rub you into a gooey mess I'd like to sleep with you.*

Ross sighed. She'd never accept—not in a hundred years.

Smart, uptight women didn't do that. Especially after five minutes of conversation.

She was uptight and she didn't look like an idiot. In fact she had the most intelligent glint in those amazing eyes. And smart, uptight girls rarely said yes to casual sex.

He thought that was tragic.

Ross decided that it would be a very good idea to get his mind out of the bedroom and back onto the purpose of this evening.

'So, tell me what you and Luc are thinking about with Win! and Bellechier.'

Ally looked at her new glass of wine and sighed. 'It's getting late... Have you eaten? My treat.' She flashed a smile. 'You might be more receptive to my suggestions on a full stomach.'

'Nice try.' But maybe dinner wasn't such a bad idea. Ross shrugged his agreement. 'Do you want to eat here or on the terrace?'

'I love the view of Table Mountain from the terrace, and I could do with some fresh air,' Ally replied, immediately slipping off her stool. 'That sounds great.'

Ross dropped his car key into the back pocket of his jeans behind his wallet and picked up both their drinks as Ally walked ahead of him. *Nice view*, he thought. *Curvy ass and long shapely legs.*

He could easily imagine his hands holding that sexy butt as her legs encircled his hips...

Down boy, he told himself. *Do try not to totally embarrass yourself.*

'So what do you think?' Ally asked, leaning across her plate as she waited for his response to her succinct top line explanation of why she thought their products could be branded together.

'No,' Ross replied, and grinned at the spark of annoyance that jumped across her face. 'Come on, Jones. I've rejected

branding opportunities from massive soft drink brands—
why would I accept *your* offer?'

Ally thought for a minute, wondering how to express the
thoughts that were tumbling around, half formed and half
baked. 'Because those other companies wanted to brand
Win! But I think I want *you*, not the game.'

Ross frowned. 'God, that sounds even worse.'

Ally pushed her plate of uneaten steak and salad away
and leaned her arms on the table. 'We wouldn't brand Win!.
We'd use you.'

'Still not getting it—and getting more scared by the moment,' Ross muttered.

'Initially I thought, like Luc, that Win! and the new Bellechier line would be a good fit. It's a sporting and lifestyle
game and our new collection is a lot more relaxed. Good
synergy.'

'Uh-huh.' Ross was looking at her as if she was about
to drop a concrete block on his head. 'Are we going to be
done with this conversation soon?'

'We were on the wrong track looking at Win!. We should
be looking at you. The man behind the game…'

Ross groaned theatrically and released a graphic swear
word. 'Sorry, but that is *such* a load of BS.'

Ally shook her head. 'It's really not. Win! is super-hot,
and anyone who is tech-savvy—which is everybody between the age of thirteen and thirty-five—would be interested in the man behind the phenomena. Who did this? How
did he do it? Add to the fact that you are…well, young, successful and a good-looking guy—'

'You think so?'

Ally draped her arm over the back of her chair and held
his eyes. 'Are you fishing for compliments now? You know
that you are hot, Bennett. We both know that you are hot.'

He lifted one eyebrow. 'Really?'

'Don't get excited; that's a professional observation.' Ally
knew that her voice held ice but she couldn't be certain that
her eyes weren't slowly undressing him. 'I also love the idea

of Crazy Collaborations—a technology think-tank—but I think that we'd have to stick to you as creator of Win! for the campaign.'

'We're not sticking to anything because the answer is still no.'

Dammit, she wasn't anywhere near changing his mind. 'What would it take?'

'To get me to do the campaign?' Ross leaned back in his chair. His mouth held a hint of a smile and his eyes narrowed in thought.

'Mmm. Come on—hit me. What would it take? What's the number? The demand? Where's the line in the sand?'

'You sure you want to know?'

Ally nodded, resigned. He was going to throw a ridiculous number out there, or ask for something stupid, impractical, unobtainable or all three. She'd been here before—matching demands with deliverability and, more importantly, deciding whether they were worth what they were asking.

Some were. Some weren't.

Ally rolled her head and looked at him from under her lashes. Oh, well, in for a penny…or for many pounds. 'Hit me.'

'I will consider doing the campaign—seriously consider it—if you sleep with me.'

Ross almost looked around, in the vague hope that someone else had suddenly joined the conversation, because he could not believe that those words had come from his own mouth. What a flippin' idiot.

He looked at Ally, who looked as shocked as he was feeling. Guppy look, Ross thought as his words registered and her eyes widened. He expected her to make a fish noise at any minute. He raked his hand through his hair. The words had slipped out. He'd been thinking them, but he normally managed to keep his thoughts behind his teeth. They were at best wildly inappropriate, and at worst sexual harassment of the worst kind.

It was pushing her into a corner, asking her to go beyond the call of duty. Of course she would say no—probably at the same time that she threw that glass of red wine in his face.

And he would so deserve it. What was he thinking? Oh, wait… Maybe he wasn't thinking…maybe he was allowing his *little* head to do the talking.

Ally just stared at him with her surprised fish face and he shifted in his chair. He wished she would say something and give him a hint of the amount of crap he'd just jumped into.

He lifted his hands in a gesture of apology. 'Sorry. That was…'

'Rude? Inappropriate? Offensive?' Ally tapped her finger against the white tablecloth.

'All of the above?'

'Damn right.'

She shrugged a slim shoulder and smiled. *Smiled?*

'Okay, let's go.'

Whoa! Stop the bus! She was prepared to do this? Had he heard her correctly? No, he couldn't have.

'Seriously?'

Those eyes bored into him. 'Wasn't it a serious offer?'

'Yes. No… Dammit, I didn't expect you to say yes!'

Ally cocked her head. 'Why not?'

'Because I didn't think that you were the type.' And, more worrying, he really didn't want her to be the type. Over the years he'd met far too many women who'd use any weapon they could, including their sexuality, to get one step higher up the corporate ladder. Grasping, greedy, power-hungry women who thought it was acceptable to sleep, lie and manipulate their way to the top.

The realist in him knew that he was a target for those predatory types. He had money, influence and, according to that stupid poll recently, power. What that meant exactly he had no damn idea, but he couldn't help feeling disappointed that Luc's sister used the same tactics.

Disappointed, yeah…but he was attracted enough, wanted her too much, not to take what she was offering.

And he *did* want to have sex with her. He wanted to see whether her eyes deepened or lightened in passion, whether she huffed or moaned her pleasure, whether her skin was as fragrant as he thought, whether those long legs could wind around his hips just as he'd imagined they could.

Ross took a sip of whisky and nearly choked when Ally stood up and draped a black leather bag over her slim shoulder. 'So, shall we go upstairs?'

'Fine.'

Ross nearly bit his tongue trying to get the word out. *Your room, my room, the lobby floor*, Ross thought in a daze. He couldn't believe that his stupid flip comment was going to lead to him getting it on with this gorgeous woman.

Utterly bemused, sure that he was operating in an alternative reality, he stumbled to his feet.

This was proof that God did, indeed, look after the intensely stupid.

How could she be both incredibly turned on and scorchingly angry? Ally wondered as she stepped into the lift ahead of Ross. She didn't have any objection to sleeping with Ross—her monologue in the Ladies' earlier was proof of that—but she despised the link between sex and her career.

How dared he make sex with her a condition of doing business? That behaviour was no longer acceptable in any circumstances! Sex was sex and work was work and the first one should never be used as a tool for negotiation. This was the twenty-first century and men didn't get away with that kind of testosterone-fuelled crap any more. And it hurt like a man-o-war sting that he thought that she was stupid enough, desperate enough, insecure enough about her job that she would even consider sleeping with him to get what she wanted from him.

She might be one or all of those things—but she'd never use her body as she would her laptop or her mobile.

As for the turned-on part—jeez, Louise. She was in a small, slow lift with a super-fine guy who twisted her panties with just one look out of those lazy gold-green eyes. Despite the fact that he was a Neanderthal, she wanted him in the worst way possible. But there was no way she could have him...*ever.*

But she *could* teach him a lesson in sexual harassment. Oh, yeah, she was going to harass the hell out of him...

Ally watched the doors close and was grateful they were the only occupants of the lift. She knew it would take about a minute to get to her floor, so she'd better get busy.

Before she could talk herself out of it she whirled around, grabbed Ross's shirt and slammed her mouth on his. His mouth opened in surprise and she took the opportunity to slide her tongue inside. Her body sighed at the heat and spice of his mouth. She opened her hands and spread her fingers across his wide chest, her palms loving the feel of hard muscles and the slow thump-thump of his heartbeat.

It took him only seconds to react, and then his hands were in her hair, and he was in charge of their kiss, and he was angling her face to tongue her deeper. One hand dropped to yank her hips against his. The hard, hard length of his erection pushed against her stomach, and she had to restrain herself from reaching down and cupping him, sliding her thumb up and across its full tip.

If she did that she'd never stop this, and she had to...

Ten seconds more, she thought as the doors slid open and the bell dinged. Ally wound her arms around his neck and tangled her tongue with his in a low, sexy swirl that had him moaning into her mouth. She withdrew and plunged again, and was only dimly aware that Ross had shoved out his hand and was holding the doors open, keeping the lift on that floor.

'I want you,' he growled in between hot, wet kisses.

'I know.'

It was now or never, Ally thought, desperate for more... so much more. If she let him get out of this lift then she'd let him into her room and she'd be flat on her back and naked before her head had stopped spinning.

She wanted to see him, explore him, taste him, touch him. But not like this. Because while she didn't need to love a guy to have sex with him she did have to like him, and there should be at the very minimum mutual respect between them.

Ally wrenched her mouth away, ducked out from under his arm and hit the close doors button before he could even react. She stepped out of the lift as the doors started to close.

'What the hell, Alyssa?' he demanded, hot eyes blazing, his hands easily pushing the lift doors open again.

'Yeah, so *not* sorry. Did you really think that I was that easy or that desperate? That I would just fall into bed with you so that I could get you to sign on the dotted line?' She gave him a frosty smile and gestured to his tented pants. 'Enjoy trying to hide *that* as you walk through the lobby... Oh, hello! Do you want me to hold the lift for you?'

Ally stepped aside to let two elderly ladies into the lift and grinned when Ross turned his back to them.

Except that now she had an eyeful of that super-fine taut ass she'd had her hands on a minute before.

Ally placed her hand on her forehead and stumbled towards her room.

This was the problem with playing with fire: you ended up getting a little scorched.

CHAPTER THREE

ALLY TOUCHED THE side of her Bellechier sports watch as she jogged up to the steps that led to the hotel's seaside entrance and placed her hands on her knees, hauling in wet air. Humid, she thought, and hot already at seven in the morning. She glanced at her watch: six miles in fifty minutes. Not her best time, but acceptable—especially since she'd tossed and turned all night and when she'd finally slept had had incredibly restless dreams.

All featuring last night's sexy jerk.

Behind her sunglasses Ally scowled at the waves smacking the beach across the road and promenade. She might have left him in an awkward position last night—good, he *so* deserved it!—but she hadn't emerged from their dizzying encounter unscathed. She'd felt tense, fidgety…*horny*, dammit.

Apart from her inability or unwillingness to connect… and her crazy work schedule…and the fact that she hadn't dated or felt attracted to any man in a long time…apart from all that she was still a reasonably normal woman in her late twenties and she did get normal urges.

Up to now she'd always been perfectly content with a bit of self-love and was easily able to sort herself out. She'd tried that last night and, like most of the few lovers she'd had, she hadn't delivered. She had just ended up feeling more frustrated and hornier than before, which sucked. Maybe it was time to cave in and buy that dildo she'd seen online. Except that now she wasn't sure that it would help. She wanted masculine fingers between her legs, a hard body above hers, the hot, thick thrust of an erection pushing into her.

She still wanted Ross and that pushed up her irritation levels. Even a long run hadn't banished her frustration; maybe a cold shower would do the trick.

Ally stood up, placed her hands on her hips and walked to the low wall that separated the beach from the promenade. Placing one foot on the low wall, she did some warm-down stretches as she watched the ships on the horizon and thought about the day ahead.

She was booked on a flight back to Geneva that night so she had the day open to do as she pleased. She could buckle down in front of her computer—as long as she had her computer she could work anywhere—and get a solid eight hours in either in her room, one of the lounges or on one of the many verandas in the hotel. That was what she should do.

Bellechier had a second store opening in Hong Kong and another in Miami, and there were countless items on her to-do list to ensure that these new additions exuded the same class and charisma as their other stores. As Brand and Image Director, it was her job to make sure that the look and feel of the new stores was everything their customers expected them to be.

Then she had magazine adverts to approve, paperwork regarding their sponsorship of a yacht race to plough through and a new face to find for the new line.

Ally wiped the perspiration from her brow before resting her forehead on her knee. She wished she was the type of person who could just pull on a bikini, grab her e-reader and towel and hit the beach—who could spend the day in the sunshine doing nothing. But that just wasn't Ally. No: she'd sit down and within a half-hour she'd be feeling guilty because she wasn't being productive, feeling tense because she'd be making mental lists of what she could be doing.

The truth was that she was happiest working; at work

she didn't have to think about anything else except the next task she had to do. Work was her entertainment. She felt safe there. It was her demanding lover. Ally looked at the beach again and sighed.

Intellectually she knew that she should want to take time off, that she was entitled to relax, to have some fun, but she couldn't translate the thought into acceptance. Working was her way of repaying her debt to Sabine and Justin; it was her way of saying thank you. She couldn't be the soul-sharing, emotionally expressive daughter they wanted—dear God, she would be if she could—so hard work was all she could give them.

She'd do anything they asked unless it involved her heart—not that she was sure she had one any more. She knew what her life could have been like, and the thought of it still made her shiver. If Sabine and Justin hadn't pulled her out of that sterile hotel room the Thai authorities and later the British Embassy had shoved her into after they'd removed her dad's body from the beach in Phuket, God knew what would have happened to her. She had no other relatives—none that she knew of anyway—and no one else would have run to her rescue.

She owed them for giving her a home and an education, but she couldn't risk loving them too much—just in case they got whipped away as well. She didn't think she could survive that.

She had to work this morning, but it would be an absolute sin not to spend some time on the beach. So…what if she printed out those reports she needed to go through on her portable printer and took them to the beach with her? She would still be working…*and* getting a tan. And since she needed to concentrate while reading them she wouldn't have time to think of Ross Bennett—the A-grade sexy dipstick.

But she'd only be productive if she didn't think of his clever mouth, his big hand on her breast, that hard thigh pressing into her crotch. Ally sighed as her skin prickled and her crotch throbbed. Casting a last look at the ocean, she turned to walk back into the hotel. *Here we go again.*

A cold shower was her last resort; if that didn't work then she was definitely ordering that sex toy.

Like most of his gender, Ross hated apologising. It made him feel stupid and weak and…stupid.

But stupid he had been, and although Ally had punished him for it—being in a lift with two nosy old ladies with a full erection had not been fun—he knew that he still owed her an apology. He'd tried most of last night and all of this morning to find a reason why he didn't, shouldn't, couldn't—and still hadn't found one.

He'd opened his big mouth and by doing so he'd screwed up, and he was enough of a man to admit it. For most of the morning he'd tried hard to ignore his conscience but at noon, when he realised that he'd achieved sweet FA, he'd given in and left his office to head over to Ally's hotel.

He needed to apologise—not only because his conscience dictated it but also because his father had never been able to do so… *Saying sorry is for wusses, pansies and pathetics.* That was one of Jonas Bennett's favourite sayings. But Ross had always vowed to be as little like his dad as possible.

Propositioning Ally in the way he had was the kind of thing his father would do: when Jonas wanted something he used any means he could to get it. Winning, getting his way, coming out on top was all that mattered to him, and last night Ross had proved that in certain ways he *was* still his father's son.

He loved and hated that fact. Loved that he had his father's drive, passion and work ethic. Hated the fact that he also had his deeply competitive streak. And his stubbornness.

His mother was either a fool or a saint for staying married to him for nearly thirty-five years. How did she do it? Love, she'd once told him, wasn't an emotion but an action.

When you'd been married as long as they had, she'd added, sometimes you had to choose to love and to fight for love.

That sounded too much like hard work, and Ross had yet to find a woman who interested him enough to consider the possibility of a lifetime with her. Ally Jones definitely wasn't a candidate. Besides, even if he was looking for 'the one', he wouldn't choose a tense, pushy, uptight corporate drone. He'd left that world behind years ago—and all the stress that went with it; why would he ever get involved with a woman deeply entrenched in it?

No, he liked to keep his personal relationships simple and above all honest. So if he hooked up with someone he always made it clear that he wasn't looking for a long-term relationship. One thing was for sure: when he *did* find Wonder Woman—he was still too busy to commit the time needed to find her—he'd never let his partner feel she had to compete with his work for his attention, as he'd had to do as a child.

Right—enough introspection. Let's get this damned apology done and dusted so I can get some work done today.

He believed Miss Jones was on the beach, the concierge told him, so Ross walked out through the doors leading to the promenade, flipping his sunglasses onto his face to hide his eyes from the blistering glare of the midday sun.

Standing at the wall, he scanned the beach, which was reasonably busy for a Thursday in September. Female faces were hidden under floppy hats, caps and sunglasses, so how was he going to find her?

By going up to every single woman on the beach and acting like a pervert, that was how. Perfect. Just what he needed.

Ross stepped onto the beach, ignoring the hot sand that crept into his flip-flops as he made his way to the most populated part of the beach. He looked out to the sea and watched as a woman walked out of the waves and pushed her wet hair back from her face.

He instantly recognised that body, its essential bits covered by fluorescent aqua triangles; he had felt it tremble under his touch last night. A waist he could span with both his hands, curvy hips, legs that went on for ever. Ross swallowed, realised that saliva had disappeared from his mouth and stood still as she strolled up to a beach blanket and dropped onto it, tipping her elfin face up to the sun.

A fist grabbed his heart and squeezed. She was utterly, maddeningly, crotch-jumpingly beautiful and he still wanted her. Probably would do anything to have her.

Just for a night…a couple of nights; just to get lost in that face, that body, the comprehensive femininity of her. And, because he'd been an utter ass, he probably never would.

That sucked.

Ross ran a hand through his hair, gestured to a beach vendor and bought two bottles of water from the elderly man. Cracking the seal on one, he took a long sip and headed to the beach blanket where Ally lay back on her elbows, smiling at two toddlers who were arguing over a spade.

He sat down next to her, handed her a bottle of water and jumped right in. 'Sorry.'

Ally took the bottle, raised her eyebrows at him and curled her lip. 'You think a cold bottle of water and a half-assed apology is going to work?'

'No.' Ross twisted his lips in frustration. 'But I thought I would give it a go.'

Ross removed the bottle from her grasp, cracked the lid for her and handed it back. 'I opened my mouth and spoke without thinking—not something I often do. I wanted to take the words back as soon as I said them.'

Ally cocked her head.

Bloody Nora, the woman had a stare that had all the power of an industrial laser. And why did that turn him on?

'Then why did you follow me up to my room?' she asked.

What? Was she kidding? Judging by her puzzled look, obviously not.

'Have you looked at yourself lately? You are seriously *hot*!' He sighed and lifted one arrogant eyebrow slowly.

'Men are simple creatures, Jones. When they hear "let's have sex" everything else goes out the window. I thought I'd hit the mother lode. Yeah, I messed up, but you were prepared to ignore that and nail me anyway. I wasn't going to turn you down. A saint couldn't—and I'm no saint.'

'I just bet you aren't,' Ally muttered, sitting up and reaching for her bag.

Pulling out a pair of sunglasses—Bellechier, slick and sexy—she pushed them onto her face and leaned back on her elbows again, bending her knees and digging her toes into the sand. Drops of water still lay on her skin, gathered in her belly button, and Ross wished he could sip the salty water from that little receptacle, slide his mouth over her flat stomach, explore the skin that covered her hipbones.

Frick, the woman could rock a bikini.

'Gorgeous day,' he mumbled, staring hard at the ships on the horizon, waiting to dock in the harbour further down the beach.

'Very.'

'So…sorry.' He thought he needed to say it again—hopefully for the final time.

Ally tipped her head back and her wet hair, curly with salt water, almost touched the sand behind her shoulderblades. 'Your apologies could use some work, Bennett.'

True. 'So I'm forgiven?'

Ally shrugged. 'Does it matter?'

It did, actually. Ross lifted one shoulder. 'I'm a straight shooter, Ally. Normally. Despite last night's mix-up, I don't play games and I don't confuse sex with business.'

Ally looked at him and he couldn't believe how relieved he felt when he caught her mouth twitching with amusement. Leaning over, he pushed her glasses down her nose and saw that her eyes were lighter, almost dancing with mischief. He felt stupidly relieved.

'What?' he asked, not entirely sure if he really wanted to know why she was smiling.

'So how long did you spend in the lift facing the wall?'

'Far too long,' he growled. 'Those wrinklies thought I was sick. They kept asking if I was all right.'

Ally grinned. She lifted the water in a toast. 'Are you expecting me to apologise?'

'For the kiss or for leaving me high and dry for the rest of the night?' Ross asked sourly. Ally gurgled and he couldn't help smiling at her infectious laughter. 'I loved the kiss and I deserved the frustration. I'm a big boy. I coped. Are we done with this now?'

Ally hiccupped a laugh. 'Oh, no, you're not getting off that easily.' She dropped her knees and sat up, pushing her glasses into her hair. '*You*, mister—' she rammed a finger into his bicep '—are going to sit through my entire presentation and you are going to seriously consider my offer.'

Ross flopped back into the sand and groaned loudly. Gorgeous and pushy...why was life punishing him like this?

She'd arrived in Cape Town yesterday and so far she'd kissed a hot man, had a swim in the Indian Ocean and spent some time in the sun, Ally thought, walking from her hotel room to the lift. That was more excitement than she'd had all year.

Catching a glimpse of her reflection in the lift doors, she nodded her head at her professional look. She felt a great deal more confident in a short flared skirt and ruffled white top; talking to Ross in that tiny bikini—the only one in her size in the hotel shop—had made her feel self-conscious and far too exposed. She'd caught the glances he gave her and been very glad she'd recently hit the salon for her monthly waxing and defoliating session. Imagine sitting there with hairy legs, fuzzy underarms and an untidy crotch—how mortifying that would have been! Ally felt herself blush and told herself not be ridiculous.

Business, Jones. Try to act professional, you moron.

Ally rolled her shoulders... It was back to business now and she would be all and only business. Ross had reluctantly agreed to take her back to RBM, where he would listen to her whole proposal for the campaign, sit through her presentation and seriously consider Bellechier's offer. She didn't know if his about-face was because he was embarrassed about his behaviour last night or because he'd rethought his position, but she didn't care. All she cared about was that she'd got a second chance to do her job—a job that she was good at—and that after this meeting she'd be able to go home to Geneva and tell Luc that she'd given it her best shot.

If Ross said no she could go on to the next candidate feeling utterly guilt-free—she'd tried. Luc would be disappointed—and that sucked—but he wasn't unfair. He knew that there were some horses—asses?—that were too ornery and too stubborn to drink when they were led to water.

Ally stepped out of the lift and her heart bumped when she saw Ross standing by the indoor fountain. His black shorts hit his knee and he wore a checked orange and white button-down shirt over a white T-shirt. He hadn't shaved. She suspected that he left his beard to grow for days until it started to annoy him and then he shaved again. She wondered what he'd look like in a suit and tie. Gorgeous, she decided. He had that tall, broad-shouldered, slim-hipped frame that would make a hessian sack look good.

Ross turned as she approached him and immediately took her laptop bag off her shoulder and gripped it in his hand. Lazy eyes started at the tips of her feet and ended on her face.

'I really, *really* prefer the bikini, Jones.'

Ally twisted her lips in annoyance but her skin flushed with pleasure. 'Can you at least try to be businesslike, Bennett?'

'But it's so much more fun making you blush.' Ross placed his hand on her lower back to guide her to the lifts that would take them to the underground parking lot and Ally sucked in her breath at his touch.

Concentrate, Alyssa.

'Are you always this serious, Jones? Do you ever cut loose, have some fun?'

No, but she'd never tell him that, she thought as Ross jabbed the button of the lift.

'Well, *do* you?' Ross pressed.

'Of course I do,' Ally lied. 'All the time. I work hard but I play harder.'

Ross's thick eyebrows rose in surprise. 'Really? And how, pray tell, do you cut loose?'

Damn, Ally thought, thinking fast. 'I dance. Latin American mostly.' It wasn't a complete lie—more like a very stretched-out truth. She had taken dance classes when she was a teenager and she'd been pretty good. Until her dance partner had declared that he couldn't dance with someone who couldn't communicate and had dumped her for a tall redhead who never shut up.

'Okay, dance. What else?' Ross said as they stepped into the open lift.

Okay, now she had to flat-out lie so that he didn't realise that she did nothing but work. She fiddled with her watch and thought hard. Dammit, what did normal people do?

'I go clubbing, meet friends for supper, go to the theatre. Movies.'

'What was the last movie you saw?' Ross leaned his shoulder into the wall of the lift, half smiling.

'Why are you interrogating me?' Ally demanded.

'Why are you lying to me?' Ross countered.

'And why would you think I'm lying?'

'Because a person who sends e-mail messages at ten-thirty on a Saturday night and leaves voice messages with me on a Sunday morning, Sunday evening and at nine p.m. on Tuesday night does *not* have a rocking social life. She might even be a bit work-obsessed. And...hmm...who *was* that person?' The lift doors opened with a ping and Ross grinned. 'Oh, wait! That was *you*. So what was the last movie you saw, Jones?'

Ally just scowled at him. *Note to self: Ross remembers small details. Dammit.*

'No comeback?' Ross asked as he escorted her across the parking lot to a clump of motorbikes next to the lift.

'I'm thinking of a polite way to tell you to a) mind your own business and b) that you are talking rubbish,' Ally replied in her coolest voice—the one she used when she wanted people to back the hell off. Desperate to change the subject, she looked around. 'Where's your car?'

Ross walked to an over-large, stygian black motorbike and fiddled with a box on the back. Flipping it open, he removed two black helmets. 'No car—just this. Put this on.'

'Of *course* you wouldn't use something as normal as a car for transport. Too pedestrian for you.'

'I like bikes,' Ross said mildly.

'I like cars.' Ally glared at the massive bike. It was muscled, sleek, oozing testosterone…just like its owner. 'This is the motorbike equivalent of one of those stupid, oversized petrol-guzzling SUVs…' She snapped her fingers in impatience. 'What are they called? Those stupid big cars that take up half of the road?'

Ross named the vehicle she was thinking of.

'That's it. So, *this* bad boy is the motorcycle equivalent of that humming car.'

Ross lifted his hand in confusion. 'What are you talking about?'

'When men buy hugely powerful machines like this, psychologists think that it's a way of them reassuring the world that they're not…*ahem*…undersized.'

Ally lifted both shoulders at Ross's shocked face. It was a little bit of payback for his earlier comments.

She widened her eyes to look sincere. 'What? It's true. I did psychology as part of my MBA in marketing.'

'You're nuts. Men don't think like that.' That sexy mouth quirked up at the corners. 'And I've never had any complaints about the size of my penis.'

'The opinions of two old ladies in a lift don't count,

Bennett,' Ally quipped, and immediately thought that she'd
gone too far.

This was not an appropriate conversation, but Ross had
a way of bringing out her inner Crazy Girl. Dear Lord she
hoped that he had a sense of humour or else she was up the
river Caca.

His loud laugh told her he did. His eyes crinkled as he
slung the computer case across her chest and plopped the
helmet over her head. 'You have a smart mouth, Ally.'

'I really do.' Ally tried to push the helmet off but his hand
held it on her head. 'And it's trying to tell you that I am not
getting on that bike. It's big and mean and dangerous. And
my skirt is too tight to get on it!'

There—that should stop the argument. She'd be a civ-
ilised person and take a taxi to RBM and meet him there.
And she'd do it without flashing her panties.

Ross held her hands in his. 'The bike is just a machine
and I control it. I'll keep you safe, I promise. As for your
skirt…' he gestured to the deserted parking lot '…nobody
will see you get on. It might hitch up an inch or two. So
what? You have great legs that deserve to be shown off.'

'Flatterer.'

'C'mon, Jones, it's a stunning day.' Ross straddled the
bike and shoved the key into the ignition. 'Cut loose. Prove
to yourself that you can.'

The sound pounded through her system and Ally licked
her lips. God, how would it feel to have that power beneath
her, between her legs?

And the motorbike would be just as good.

'You won't regret it, I promise. Stop being uptight and
prissy and get on.'

'I am not uptight and prissy,' Ally muttered, knowing
that she was and wishing she wasn't. Dammit, was she really going to do this? It seemed she was—if only to show
Mr Cool that she could be cool.

Although she guessed that he wasn't that easily fooled.

'Don't peek.'

'Wouldn't dream of it,' Ross assured her. 'Throw your leg behind me and put your arms around my waist. When we're on the road just move with me. Don't fight me or we will crash. I move—you move. Got it?'

Ally heaved in a breath. 'Got it.'

'Trust me?'

Funnily enough, she did. 'Yes. Eyes forward and don't peek!'

Ally hitched her skirt up and threw her leg over the bike and sighed as the leather made contact with the inside of her thighs. Then she slid down the bike and her thighs gripped Ross's hips as her breasts slammed against his broad back. Lust and heat and warmth instantly dialled her panties up from warm to fire-hot.

'Jones?'

Instinctively Ally glanced over his shoulder to his left side mirror and her eyes connected with his warm, heated gaze. 'What?'

'I really, really like your red panties. Colour suits you.'

Ally punched his shoulder blade. 'You sod! I told you not to peek!'

Ross laughed, and the rest of her protests were lost under the roar of the motorbike.

CHAPTER FOUR

'No.'

Ally, who'd finished her presentation, run through the figures and answered Ross's many questions, wasn't surprised by his refusal. From the moment she'd met him and decided that he'd be perfect for the campaign she'd known that he'd be a hard sell. He was one of those men who really didn't need the ego boost the campaign would provide and, honestly, there wasn't much of an incentive for him to do it.

Win! was doing stupendously well anyway, unlike celebrities he didn't need his face on billboards and the small screen to keep his profile up, and he certainly didn't need the cash they'd pay him.

To be honest, she wasn't in the least surprised that he'd turned her down.

What else could she say? Do? Offer her body again? It was tempting…

Ally scratched the top of her head with her pen and swivelled her head round when the door to Ross's office opened and a creature she fervently hoped was a dog entered the room.

'He's all yours, Ross.' A young man wearing sunglasses and baggy shorts dropped a leash onto the coffee table next to Ally as the half-dog, half-cow trotted over to her and shoved its snout into her crotch.

Well, hello there.

Ross and the young man lunged forward to drag him

away but Ally shook her head, grabbed the jowly face and lowered her face to look into the dark mischievous eyes.

'You are a big, big boy and it's very rude to get that fresh on a first date, mister,' she crooned, gently rubbing his ears. 'But you *are* beautiful—even if you are the size of a spaceship.'

The dog put a ginormous paw on her thigh and Ross saw Ally's wince at the pressure. He issued a sharp command and the paw dropped back to the floor. 'Sorry. He'd climb up into your lap if you let him. He's a big baby, really.'

So this was a surprise, Ross thought. Most people—men and women—would have pushed themselves into the back of the chair to get away from sixty-five kilos of muscled, slobbery dog. Ally—supposedly uptight and tense—had just melted as she instantly bonded with his dog.

Exactly the opposite of what he'd expected her to do.

Ross watched as she pulled her nails along the front of his chest and was certain that Pic's eyes rolled back in pleasure.

'Mmm…either you don't get any love and attention here or you're a big, fat slut,' she murmured.

'He's a slut,' Ross confirmed. 'If I'm not around he begs for affection—and snacks—from anyone and everyone in the building.' Ross glanced up at the young man who was still standing at the door. 'Thanks, Guy. Can you run him tomorrow same time?'

'Sure,' Guy agreed.

Guy's eyes had widened at the love-fest happening between Pic and Ally and Ross shrugged. They both knew that Pic took his own sweet time warming to people, so this was very unusual behaviour indeed.

'What breed is he? Some sort of mastiff?' Ally asked as Guy shut the door behind him.

'Neapolitan mastiff,' Ross answered, impressed. 'A blue, because his coat has that blue sheen.'

'Does he have a name?' Ally asked as Pic rested his jowls—and there were many of them—on her bare knee.

'He has many, but the breeders named him Piccolo. I mostly call him Pic.'

Ally took a moment to make the connection and when she did she laughed out loud, dimples flashing. 'Piccolo is Italian for small. Somebody's idea of a joke?'

'He was the runt of the litter,' Ross explained. 'They never expected him to be half the size of his siblings, but he's turned out to be the best of the bunch. The breeders keep hinting that they'd like him back.'

Ally covered Pic's ears so that he couldn't hear his words. 'Don't say that in front of him,' she chided. 'You'll make him feel insecure.'

Ross laughed at her goofiness. 'He's a dog, not a child, Jones.'

Ally stroked his crinkled face and Pic sighed. 'Ignore him, darling, you and I both know that you are a fur person. You said you *mostly* call him Pic? What else do you call him?'

'It varies and very much depends on whether he's eaten another pair of my shoes, the carpet, or the pipes in the pool. *Some choice swear words* usually spring to mind,' Ross said on a smile.

'Poor baby.'

Ross let her words drift over him. 'Thank you. I've got about six left flip-flops at home. Why can't he eat the flip of a pair if he's already eaten the flop? Why does he have to start on a new pair?'

'I was actually speaking to Pic, not you,' Ally said, her hand on Pic's massive neck.

'Oh.'

Pic yawned, flopped to the ground at Ally's feet, rested his massive head on his equally massive paws and closed his eyes. Ally felt like doing the same. Instead, she tossed her pen onto the coffee table between them, stood up and stepped over Pic and looked out through the floor-to-ceiling glass wall, past the walkway that meandered around the four sides of the building and gave access to the offices on this floor and the craziness of the main floor below them.

To her, his office set-up was utterly bizarre. In the indoor quad below there were couches and huge TV screens playing music videos. Headphoned people played video games in front of another enormous wide TV screen. Very few people worked at desks, laptops seemed to be the popular choice, and his staff lounged in couches or chairs tapping at their keyboards.

The occasional mini rugby ball sailed across heads from one side of the light-filled room to the other, and weirdly dressed people with bright hair, tattoos and piercings sat at a bar in the corner, drinking coffee and chugging energy drinks.

A pot-bellied pig snored at the BDSM-booted feet of a girl with bright pink hair and tattoos—she looked about sixteen, with Goth make-up—who was having a ferocious argument with a Sheldon-lookalike nerd.

It was a crazy set-up and she'd go nuts if she had to work here. It was too busy, too chaotic, but it seemed to suit Ross perfectly.

'How do Pic and the pig get along?' she asked.

'They've learnt to tolerate each other,' Ross answered.

'I think Pink-Haired Girl is about to stab Sheldon Look-alike with a letter-opener.'

Ross stood up to see where she was looking and shook his head. 'No letter-openers. We are mostly a paper-free environment. And Kate and Hardy always argue—that's why they are really good partners. They bring out the best in each other.'

Ally shook her head in disbelief. 'She just threw her can of soda at him.'

Ross shrugged. 'He must like it since they've been married for three years.'

'*Married?* You're kidding me!'

'Nope. They are also two of the most exciting game designers I have ever met. Kate is stunningly creative and she pushes Hardy to get him to translate her visions, characters and stories for a game into code. He says he can't do it and she nags him until he does.'

Ross picked up her Bellechier fountain pen and rolled it between his fingers.

She couldn't work in an environment like this. She liked quiet, class, structure. This would be too weird—too 'out there' for her. The noise, the movement, the fizzing energy would drive her nuts. 'How do they concentrate?'

Ross leaned his shoulder into the glass. 'When I hire new people I find out how they like to work. Some people like privacy and quiet, and some—like these lot—need noise. If I need the skill and they need quiet I make that happen. Next to the refreshment bar is a door that leads to another wing of this building where there are a series of offices where quietness and sanity prevail. My second-in-command and my quiet-loving staff, and the accounts people, work out of there. They have their own entrance so that don't have to deal with the rabble.'

Ally couldn't help smiling at the amusement in his voice. 'You love the craziness, the rabble?'

Ross lifted a shoulder. 'I admire anyone who thinks outside the box, who isn't scared to be themselves—even if that self is a pink-haired, potbellied-pig-loving, tattooed creature with more holes in her skin than a sieve. Everyone just wants a place where they can do what they love to do and be who they are. For these people RBM is that place.'

Ross's look heated her skin.

'And *you* love the corporate world.'

'I do—probably as much as you hate it,' Ally agreed.

She walked back to the desk, shut down her laptop and closed the lid. Pulling herself back to the reason she was there, she sucked in her bottom lip and thought she'd try once more.

'Is there anything I can do or say that would get you to change your mind about the campaign?'

The words danced between them and Ally squeezed her eyes shut when she realised what she'd said.

She held up her hand as heat spread up her neck and into her face. 'I cannot believe I said that…again.'

Ross's laugh was low and perfectly suited for the bedroom. 'I try not to repeat past mistakes.'

'Now that you've seen what is involved and what we want, any suggestions about who else we can approach?' Ally slumped back down into a chair. 'Because if you're not going to do it then I am utterly stuck. Up the creek without a paddle.'

'C'mon, Ally, there must be tons of people who can be your face.'

'You'd think,' Ally said glumly. 'But Luc wants "different" and you were our bad-ass CEO.'

Ross laughed at that. 'Seriously? Jeez!'

He linked his hands across his stomach and watched her with those intense eyes.

'You have a tiny frown that appears between your eyes when you're stressed or thinking.' He rubbed the area between his own brows to demonstrate. 'Why is this one campaign so important? Surely this happens often?'

Ally took her time answering his question, deciding how much to tell him. 'It's the first campaign I'm fully in charge of—the first since my promotion to Brand and Image Director a couple of months ago—and I'd like it to be fabulous. Secondly, this is a brand-new line and it's crucial that it flies. Bellechier hasn't launched a new line in years—new products yes; an entire new brand, no. We suspect that we've lost our younger clients to trendier labels and this is our way to get them back.'

'So no pressure?' Ross said, deadpan.

'No pressure.' Ally, not wanting to leave him just yet, looked for a way to keep their conversation going. 'Tell me about your think tank.'

Ross explained how the project worked—that designers and inventors from all over the world submitted their ideas and concepts to a panel of experts and if, after investigation, a project seemed feasible, they were invited to Cape Town to spend some time on the top floor, working on their project. The foundation picked up their salaries and living expenses and provided them with the specialised equipment they needed for a limited time.

'It's a damn expensive exercise, though; I need to go looking for additional funding as some of the projects I'd like to explore need equipment we don't have and I can't fund through RBM,' he added, wincing. 'I hate fundraising... I'd rather have my legs waxed.'

'Hmm...' Ally touched the top of her lip with her tongue as an idea took shape in her mind. His think tank needed money. She knew of a foundation that had money. He just had to do one little thing for her...

'So let me get this straight... You will talk to your foster father, who heads up the Bellechier Foundation, and tap him for funding for my think tank if I agree to be the face for your campaign?' Ross asked, after she'd explained that she had a solution that would work for all of them.

Ally smiled at his grumpy statement. 'Pretty much.'

'Blackmail is still blackmail, even if it's wrapped up in a sparkling bow, Jones.'

Ally grinned. Blackmail? What a harsh word! 'I call it scratching each other's backs,' she replied.

Ross looked sceptical. 'And what chance do I have of getting funding from the Bellechier Foundation?'

'Oh, I'll tell them it's a condition of you being the face. Luc wants you; I want you. You want funding and the foundation funds. The foundation is family-run, and if Justin likes the project he'll fund it. Lucky for you that he loves technology,' Ally said blithely, feeling like a serene swan on the surface of the water but paddling like hell underneath.

She was so close—so damn close...

Ross pushed the pads of all his fingers into his forehead. 'Are you going to pull any other rabbits out of your hat today?' he demanded, sounding irate.

'You never know.' *Just say yes, Ross. Come on. Three letters, one syllable...*

'You secure the funding. I'll do it.'

Ross named a figure and Ally forced herself not to react—not because the figure was sky-high but because it wasn't. Jeez, that wasn't even *half* of what they'd pay him to be the face. Despite his many offers of co-branding it was clear that Ross had never got as far as discussing how much his game and his face were worth...which was far more millions than he thought.

And if the foundation didn't cough up, then Bellechier itself would. Ross simply didn't understand how valuable he was to them. His appeal was enormous: to women because he was hot, to men because he had the cool factor, and to the intellectuals, geeks and nerds because he was so damn smart.

'I'm sure we could push that figure up,' Ally said to sweeten the pot. 'Like double or triple it.'

Ross's eyes widened with surprise. 'Seriously?'

'Yes. So, do we have a deal?'

'You secure me the funding and then we have a deal.' Ross glanced at his watch and walked over to his desk. He scribbled something on a piece of paper and picked up his razor-thin laptop. 'I have a conference call in ten minutes with Japan...in the boardroom. When are you flying out?'

'This evening on the ten o'clock flight.'

Ross gestured to his office. 'Stay here and get me a formal offer before you fly. You do that and we're in business.'

Ally forced herself not to punch the air in jubilation. She'd done it...holy smoke, she had her face.

And what a gorgeous, sexy face it was! *Whoop!*

Pic, sensing her excitement, stood up and shoved his nose up her skirt. Ally squealed, and then laughed at the cold nose on her inner thigh. Pushing his face away, she dropped into the couch and wrapped her arms around his enormous neck.

Ross moved towards her and got down on his haunches next to Pic's head and ran a lazy hand down his dog's back. 'I've got to go. Get me that offer—and don't let this hustler con you into giving him any food.'

'I don't know where his food is,' Ally pointed out.

Ross stood up. 'He does.' He slapped a bright green sticky note onto her forehead with a crooked smile. 'Wireless code. I'll be a couple of hours. If you want anything to eat or drink dial nine and ask Grace for whatever you need. She'll also take Pic out if he needs to go. Get me that offer, Jones.'

Ross had always thought that he had a fairly impressive concentration span and an ability to get things done, but he was a rank amateur compared to Alyssa Jones. His conference call with Japan had taken ninety minutes and when he'd returned to his office Ally had been on her mobile, pacing his office and speaking in rapid and very expressive French. She and his damn dog had barely noticed his return, both of them lost in their own little worlds. Pic's eyes had never left her face and Ally had been utterly absorbed in her own conversation.

When she'd sat down in his large, comfortable leather chair behind his desk and propped her sexy feet up on his desk, doodling on his desk pad, he'd realised that he'd lost his office and decided to go and check what was happening in the Pit. At least people would talk to him there.

In the Pit he'd got sucked into a heated discussion about the post-apocalyptic world his designers were creating and had had to mediate a vicious argument around zombies and ghouls. Then he'd brainstormed a storyboard with Kate, ignored Hardy when he'd told them that what they wanted was impossible, and then slipped out of the noisy quad and into the silence of the quiet wing to catch up with Eli.

It was nearly three hours later now, as he sprinted up the stairs back to his office, and the Pit was all but empty. He looked at his watch and was surprised to see that it was just after six. While it wasn't unusual for his staff to work late, Friday night was party night and they moved their 'craziness', as Ally called it, to the local pub down the road.

Sometimes he joined them, sometimes not—but especially not when he was negotiating a deal with a sexy, dainty shark in heels. Yesterday there had not been a damn thing she could have said to convince him to be the new Bellechier face and yet here he was, about to look over an offer to do exactly that. She'd found his weak spot, exploited it, and was set to get exactly what she wanted.

Determined, persistent and very, very smart. He'd have to watch this one, he thought. And that wouldn't be a hardship either. God, she was lovely, Ross thought, standing in the doorway and watching as Ally's hands flew over the keyboard of her laptop. Her mobile was still surgically attached to her ear.

Her hair had half fallen out of its knot at the back of her head and her make-up had faded, allowing him to see more of those delightful freckles and her lush, unpainted mouth. The top button of her shirt had come undone, and if he tipped his head just so he could see the swell of her breast, the edges of a pale pink bra. She looked tired, he thought as she massaged her temple with her right hand, her left still tapping the keyboard. Tired, determined, and sexy as hell.

He wanted her more than he wanted his next breath. It was a damn good thing that she was climbing onto a plane tonight, because if she wasn't then he'd make another stab at sleeping with her. She'd probably shoot him down in flames but she was worth the risk…

He hadn't felt this hot, this needful of a woman, in months—possibly years.

She glanced up at him, gave him a little wave and made an effort to get up from his desk. He waved her back down and grabbed his note pad.

Food? he scrawled, and slapped the note down in front of her.

Ally held up her finger, asking him for a minute, and he

perched on the edge of his desk, waiting for her to finish her conversation. After she'd said *au revoir* she pulled her fingers away from the keyboard, yanked her headset off her ear and tossed it onto the desk.

'Hi,' she said, and he heard the weariness in her voice, saw it in the slump of her shoulders.

'Hi, back. Tough afternoon?'

'Brutal.' She held up her hand in apology. 'I don't have an offer for you yet. I've spent the afternoon tracking Luc down; I can't reach Justin. Luc is going to brief his father so I just have to wait for the decision.'

'Okay. When do you think that will be?'

Ally looked at her watch. 'Honestly…? Justin will want to do some research before throwing the foundation's money at you. Probably not until Monday morning at the earliest. Luc suggested that I stay in Cape Town until we get an answer.'

'Huh…' Ross picked up the Rubik's cube that he kept on his desk and idly turned a few layers, adding a red side to the green and yellow sides he'd already accomplished. 'So—food. What do you feel like?'

Ally leaned forward in her chair—no, *his* chair—and held her face in her hands. 'You don't look worried at all,' she commented.

What was there to worry about? he wondered. 'That's because I'm not.' He put the Rubik's cube down and folded his arms. 'Your father is either going to go for it or not; I can't influence his decision one way or the other. If he doesn't I don't get to dress up in poncey—'

'Careful…' Ally warned him.

He smiled before continuing. 'Poncey clothing and goof around in front of a camera. On the negative side, I'll have to do some fundraising. It's all good, Jones.'

'For you, maybe,' Ally grumbled. 'If he doesn't say yes then I am still short of a face.'

'Yet the world keeps turning.' Ross stretched as he stood up. 'Food! I'm starving.'

Pic's ears pricked up and he lumbered to his feet.

Ross dropped his hand and rubbed Pic's head. 'And there's the magic word. Come on—let's go, Jones.'

Ally shook her head and gave him that brief, impersonal smile he was coming to hate. It was soulless, perfunctory, and very, very corporate.

'Thanks but I am just going to go back to the hotel and order Room Service; I still have work to do.'

Seriously? On a Friday night? Who worked on a Friday night…? Ah, yes. Crazy people, workaholics and his father. And Ally Jones, apparently.

'Seriously? You're going back to your hotel to *work*?'

He deliberately made it sound like a different kind of four-letter word.

'Yep.' Ally closed down her computer, packed it into her laptop bag and refused to look at him. She stood up, shoved her feet back into her silly, sexy shoes and looked over his messy desk to see if there was anything she'd left behind. 'Right—ready to go…' She scrunched up her face in annoyance. 'Dammit, I keep forgetting that I can't step outside and expect a taxi to come whizzing by. I need to call for one.'

And that would take a while. 'I'll take you back to your hotel,' Ross offered.

'It's too far, Ross, and I've taken too much of your time already. You probably have a date or something and I'll make you late. If you can just call a taxi for me I'll wait outside.'

'That's not going to happen.' Ross waited while she preceded him out of the office, then switched off his lights and followed her down the stairs.

'I should've just rented a car…now I'm going to put you out,' Ally muttered. 'That's the problem with impulsive decisions—they just come back and bite you in the butt.'

'Mmm… And imagine what would've happened if you'd slept with me—impulsively, of course!' Ross said, his words as dry as kindling. He caught the look of horror that flashed across her face and rolled his eyes. 'That's a joke, Ally! Jeez! Do you always make a mountain out of a molehill?'

'No. Maybe. Sometimes…' Ally admitted, and Ross was surprised by her honesty.

'So, pizza and then hotel?' he asked, pushing his luck.

'Just hotel,' Ally said as they left the building.

Well, it had been worth a try.

CHAPTER FIVE

ALLY HEARD THE knock on her hotel room door, pushed her chair back from the desk and wondered who was bothering her at five-fifteen on a Saturday afternoon. She hadn't ordered Room Service and nobody but Ross knew she was in Cape Town.

Ross...it could only be.

Ally licked her lips and wished her heart would get the message and not go all fluttery and stupid and...and *girly*... whenever she thought of him. It was just...silly.

Ally looked down at her outfit: sensible beige Capri pants that finished midthigh and a black crop top that ended two inches above the waistband and showed off the straps of her purple and black push-up bra.

Not the most seductive outfit in the world.

He knocked again and Ally crossed the room to open the door. Ross, dressed in bottle-green board shorts, a white T-shirt and flip-flops that showed signs of being chewed upon, stood in her doorway. He looked rumpled and sexy and desire roared through her body.

He was standing in the entrance to her room and it was all she could to not yank him inside and climb all over him.

Ally folded her arms. 'Um... Ah... I didn't expect to see you here...I mean again—at least not until Monday when I...you know...'

Jeez, smooth. Like...not.

She took a deep breath and gathered her scattered wits

together. It took a while because some of her wits were eyeing his mouth, others were imagining his ass beneath her hands and the sluttier wits were checking out his package, which looked very impressive indeed.

She eventually managed to string a complete sentence together. 'What are you doing here?'

Ross's mouth quirked up at the corners. 'Grab some shoes and let's go.'

'Where to?' Ally asked, and then twisted her lips. 'I mean…I can't, Ross.'

'That wasn't actually a suggestion. I'm going out to listen to a jazz band and you're coming with me,' Ross countered.

'Ross, seriously—thank you for the offer, but no.'

'Okay, then.' Ross pushed past her, sat on the edge of her bed and flopped backwards. 'Let's stay here and neck. That sounds like an even better plan.'

Ally flushed, unable to take her eyes off his large, masculine frame. That was the best idea she'd heard in weeks. She could just walk on up between his spread open legs, lower herself down onto his wide chest and sip at that stunning mouth. Those impressive arms would keep her anchored as she moved against his erection…

'One of these days I'm going to be part of your daydreams, Jones,' Ross promised, his eyes molten gold.

Ally snapped back at his words and silently screamed when a deep, dark flush spread up her neck and into her face.

'Will you please leave?' she demanded, her voice hoarse.

'Go out or stay in—your choice,' Ross countered. 'I vote for staying in.'

Ally rubbed her forehead with her hand and wished that Ross had even a slight acquaintance with the word *no*. Devil and deep blue sea, she thought. If she went out with him then she'd have to talk to him, and she was already, very grudgingly, fascinated with the man. Spending more time with him, talking to him, would make her more so.

If they stayed here they'd end up having sex, which would

be beyond stupid. He would, she just knew it, be an amazing lover, and she also knew that he had the potential to become deeply addictive.

And she couldn't let that happen...

He crept into her thoughts more often than was healthy and they hadn't even got to making love yet. She was trying to avoid being alone with him because it seemed to be the intelligent thing to do, but Fate was making this so damn hard! She was drawn to Ross in a way that scared her, because no penis-toting human had ever had the impact on her that he did.

Dear Lord... Ally swayed where she stood, befuddled and bemused. Ross snapped her out of her daze when he stood up, walked over to her and gently pushed a strand of hair off her face.

'Look outside... It's a stunning spring evening: warm and soft. Everyone is outside except you. We'll take Pic for a walk along the promenade—at the moment he's entertaining, or maybe terrifying, the reception staff downstairs. We can have a couple of drinks and some food, listen to good jazz. We won't even have to talk if you don't want to. Just take a break from the small screen for a while, okay?'

How was she supposed to resist that low, sexy voice and that tempting, charming look? Ally felt herself wavering. It *was* Saturday night and she'd had a hell of a week. She could probably do with some sunshine—and when last had she breathed fresh air?

Her brain capitulated but her entire body whimpered in protest. It wanted to stay in and play with the big girl's toy in front of her...

'Okay, maybe for a little while.' Ally grabbed her bag off the couch and moved towards the door, needing to leave the room before she did something really stupid—like stripping naked and throwing herself at him.

'Jones?'

Ally, her hand on the door handle, turned to look back at him. 'Yeah?'

Ross pointed at her bare feet. 'Shoes would be a good idea.'

Ally and Ross walked down to the promenade that ran from Sea Point past Bantry Bay and all the way up to Mouille Point. As Ross had pointed out, *everybody* was outside: pensioners, teenagers, cyclists, joggers, lovers and dog-lovers walking their fur people.

Pic ambled along next to Ross, and Ally wondered who was walking who as Pic explored the exciting smells on the boardwalk and they followed his zig-zag path.

Ross bought them ice cream and she licked and sighed, happy to feel the still warm dipping sun on her bare shoulders and face. 'Where are the jazz players?' she asked.

'At a pub a little further down. What sort of music do you like?'

Okay, that wasn't too personal. Music….what did she like? She had to think for a minute. 'Modern country,' she said eventually on a huge sigh, knowing that she was about to be mocked.

She wasn't wrong. Ross looked as if he'd just found a dairy worm in his cone. 'Dear God, *why*?' he asked, utterly pained.

'The songs normally have a story; I like stories,' Ally replied.

'Frig, you need help. Hard rock, indie, even house—but *country*?'

Ally was about to tell him exactly what he could do with his help when her mobile rang. She pulled it out of the back pocket of her Capri pants and squinted at the display. 'Tante Sabine.' She sighed.

'Aren't you going to answer it?' Ross demanded.

'Maybe later.' Ally said, tucking the phone away again. She and Sabine both had the latest smartphones and all the Bellechiers liked the video calling facility. Ally hated it, because they could tell when she was where she shouldn't be—mostly in her office, but on this occasion with Ross. She was in the company of a good-looking guy on a Saturday afternoon and that would raise a lot of pesky questions from her nosy foster mum.

Ross ate the rest of his ice cream and didn't refuse when Ally offered him her half-eaten cone to finish. 'How long have you known your foster mother? How old were you when you were fostered?' he asked between bites.

Ally licked the top of her lip. 'I was fifteen when they fostered me, but I've known them my entire life. Their second oldest son and I are the same age and we were in the same class. I spent most afternoons in their house with them.'

'And you call her Tante? That's aunt, right?'

Ally wished the world would open her up and swallow her. While she'd kept lecturing herself about not probing into Ross's life, she hadn't considered that he might probe into hers.

'Why hasn't she been upgraded to Mum, Ally?'

She had asked her to, about six months after her dad had died, but she hadn't been ready to make that step. She hadn't ever asked her again, and Ally had been too scared to raise the subject in case they were happy to keep the status quo.

Her mobile rang again, and of course it was Sabine...

'Where are you?' she demanded in French.

'Walking along a promenade in Cape Town,' Ally replied in the same language, looking down at the screen and seeing her face.

'By yourself?' Sabine demanded.

Ally's eyes flew to Ross and she didn't see Sabine's quick smile of delight. 'I'm with Ross Bennett,' she said eventually, and turned the phone so that Sabine could see Ross. Ross grinned down at her and Sabine smiled slowly.

The flirt.

As she'd thought, Ross could melt any woman's panties,

regardless of age, at fifty paces. This was why his was the best face to launch the new Bellechier line.

'*Bonjour, madame.*'

The words were polite but the inflection was pure, *Hey, sweetheart...*

'Ross Bennett. Thank you for showing my...' Sabine's eyes flicked to Ally and quickly away again. '...Alyssa Cape Town.'

He'd like to show her a lot more than just Cape Town, but Ross was pretty sure that Sabine Bellechier didn't need to know that. On the other hand, judging by her approving look and the twinkle in her eyes, she might approve and cheer him on.

As Ally and Sabine chatted away—in English, for his benefit—he wondered what the deal was between these two. They acted like mother and daughter, had the same crazy, jump around, finish-each-other's-sentence conversations that he remembered his sister and his mum having, and they very obviously adored each other. So why were they both so damn scared to take the step and acknowledge the mother-daughter bond that was so tangible he could almost taste it?

Families were...*weird*, he thought. And he couldn't judge—his was as screwed up as any.

He turned his concentration back to their conversation when he heard his name mentioned.

'Ross, my husband Justin would like me to pass on the message that he has no problem making a donation on behalf of the Bellechier Foundation to your think tank project in exchange for you being the face of the new campaign. I trust that is acceptable to you?'

'It depends how much he wants to give Crazy Collaborations, *madame.*'

'I think you will be happy with the amount he intends to offer, Ross,' Sabine said, her face serious. 'You will have a formal offer on your desk first thing Monday morning. If you accept it, Alyssa will bring it back to Geneva with her and the contracts will follow.'

'Let me see what the offer looks like and we can take it from there,' Ross said, totally unfazed. 'Thank you.'

Ally and Sabine chatted for a minute longer and then Ally disconnected, pushed her mobile into her pocket and slipped her sunglasses back onto her face. 'Sabine—matriarch of the Bellechiers.'

'She seems nice.'

'She is. What's your mother like?'

Ross jammed his hands into the pockets of his basketball shorts. 'Bubbly…loving…fussy. Lonely.'

Ally's eyes sharpened at that comment and Ross hissed a mild curse for letting the words slip out.

She was too sharp to let it slide. 'Lonely? Why?'

Ross stared out to sea. 'My dad is very driven, very ambitious. He's a compulsive workaholic and, while he loves my mum, work always comes first with him. My mum gets the crumbs of his attention.'

As we did. All our lives. Unless we joined the family business. Then we were golden until we left and became nothing.

Harsh, but true. And that was why he would never allow work to consume him or become emotionally involved with anybody who allowed work to consume her life. He was never, ever going back to playing the cymbals in the orchestra of his life again.

Which reminded him…

He steered Ally towards his favourite pub and shook his head in dismay. 'Country music? Seriously?'

Being alone with him was dangerous, Ally thought, as she shoved her keycard into the slot to pop open the door to her hotel room. But instead of saying goodnight in the doorway she allowed Ross to follow her into her dark room.

He walked over to the small sitting area and flipped on a lamp that cast a golden light over the room.

Jeez, she'd even settle for Pic as a chaperone right now, but Ross had unfortunately dropped him off at his house before bringing her back to her hotel.

'I liked the pub. Nice place...nice music,' Ally gabbled, *so* conscious of him standing there, looking at her as if he wanted to slurp her up just as he had that ice cream earlier.

'Mmm. Not that I could concentrate on a damn thing,' Ross responded, walking across the room to where she still stood by the door. What did he mean by that?

He placed one finger under the strap of her bag and gently pulled if off her shoulder. It dropped to the floor with a muted thud.

'Shall we order some wine from Room Service?' he asked, his hand rubbing her from shoulder to wrist in a gesture that soothed as much as it aroused.

'No, thanks. I'm buzzing as it is.' Ally made herself step away and walked over to open a window, hoping that the breeze would cool her down and bring her the common sense she needed to resist him.

She *had* to resist him; they had business to do and she couldn't jeopardise it now. It was too important...

All thoughts of work fled when his hands gripped her shoulders and pulled her into him, her back to his chest, his arm diagonally across her chest. She couldn't help sighing, resting her cheek against his bicep.

Ross cupped one hip in his hand. 'So you liked the jazz, huh?'

'It was better than I expected,' Ally admitted, feeling his fingers spreading across her stomach.

His erection was hard and unapologetic against her back and she struggled to keep her hands from reaching back and feeling him; she wanted to know him up close and personal.

Very, *very* personal.

'Sweetheart, anything is better than country music.'

'Don't knock it until you've tried it.'

Ally tried to interject some feistiness into her voice but her words just came out low and sexy. She felt loose and warm and very, very relaxed. And Ross's fingers drawing figures of eight on her hip were making sparks run along her nerve-endings straight to her lady parts.

'Let me stay tonight,' Ross murmured.

Ally looked at his reflection in the glass and saw her lust reflected in his eyes.

'I can't. We shouldn't.'

'Why not?' Ross asked, his words fluttering against the cord in her neck.

'Because we are doing business.' Ally managed to find the words, to force them out. 'Nothing is concluded, settled. I don't want you to think that I use sex…'

Ross swore. 'The other night proved that you don't.'

'But still…' Ally tipped her head back as Ross's lips nibbled on her jaw. 'Besides, I'm not…'

Ross's mouth stopped its exploration and he waited for her to continue. When she didn't he filled in the silence. 'Not ready? Too soon?'

Ally nodded, thankful that he was astute enough to pick up on what she was feeling without her having to say the words.

Ross turned her around, keeping his eyes locked on hers as he pulled the band from her ponytail, swept his fingers through her hair, raking strands off her face.

'You are so beautiful,' he murmured as her hair fell to her shoulders to spill over the fabric of her T-shirt.

Ally watched, mesmerised, as his fingers danced down her throat and over her chest. Ross buried his face into the curve of her neck as he cupped her breasts, easily covering them with his big, broad, dangerous hands. Then she remembered that they shouldn't be doing this and she stiffened.

Ross rubbed her nipple with his thumb. 'Relax, Al. Nothing is going to happen that you don't want to. Trust me.'

She lifted her arms to curl them around his neck, lifting her breasts higher and forcing her nipples into his palms. Ross responded by rubbing his thumbs over the hard nubs, lazily watching her eyes fog up. He bunched the bottom of her shirt in his fist and pulled it upwards, gradually revealing her flat stomach and her chest to his appreciative gaze. He looked at her see-through lace bra with obvious appreciation.

'Oh, yeah…' he muttered, ducking his head and placing his lips over her lace-covered nipple, drawing it into his mouth, lightly nipping it with his teeth and soothing the flicker of pain with his clever tongue.

Above his head Ally moaned, clasped his head and held it to her breast. Ross responded by slipping his hand between her legs and unerringly finding her sweet spot through the layers of her clothes.

'God, Ross…' Ally murmured. 'That feels so good.'

'I know, honey.'

Ross pulled her shirt up and over her head. Then he pulled the cup of her bra aside and tasted her nipple without the barrier of lace while he slid down her Capris and pushed them over her hips so that they ended up in a pile around her feet.

Ally tried to protest, but then his hand was in her panties, sliding through her strip of pubic hair and into her slit, touching her clit with his thumb. She yelped, and then one long finger pushed into her tight passage.

Ally let out another yelp of piercing pleasure. 'God, Ross, we should stop,' she panted, even though her hips were pushing down on his finger, his thumb, demanding more. She almost cried when Ross pulled out of her, but then his two hands were on her hips and she was lifted and carried to the desk, where he pushed her laptop out of the way to make room for her.

'Not a chance,' Ross stated, spreading her knees apart with his thigh. With one quick twist the ties of her G-string snapped and he pulled the triangle away from her so that it fell from the desk, revealing her to his hot and heated gaze.

'As I said…beautiful.'

'Ross…' Ally muttered, squirming against the cold wooden desk, desperately—selfishly—wanting him to resume what he'd been doing.

Instead of touching her down below, he touched his lips to the corner of her mouth. 'What do you need, baby?'

'What you were doing… I shouldn't ask because I can't… won't… We shouldn't…' Ally spoke, but she was not sure if she was making sense. She just wanted him touching her so knowingly, so perfectly.

'You want more?'

Ally placed her hands on the desk behind her and arched her back as his finger rolled down the column of her throat, down her chest and across one nipple.

'Do you want me to touch you?'

'Yes! God, it's been so long.'

Ally dropped her head back as that finger—that knowing, amazing, lightning-infused finger—explored her belly button, went lower, touched her bead and slid into her hot, wet, demanding passage. Then a second finger joined the first, and his tongue swirled into her panting mouth as he stroked her bead, and she launched herself up and shouted with embarrassing abandon.

She pumped and he kissed; he stroked and she whirled away on a starburst of pleasure. Until a dazzling display of fireworks erupted from her innermost core. Colours swirled and twirled and she danced in them until they fizzled and died, and then she slumped in Ross's arms, her face in his neck, as she tried to suck in air.

Ross pulled his hand out from between her legs and held her head against his neck, his hand sticky on her thigh.

'Dear God…' Ally murmured when she had enough air for words.

'That good, huh?' Ross dropped a brief kiss on her temple.

Then she realised that he was still standing between her legs, fully dressed and very hard. She rested her hands on his pecs, feeling the thud-bump of his heartbeat under her hands.

'You—are we?—can I—?' Ally tripped and stumbled over her words, inwardly cursing herself for being so inexperienced, so damn gauche. And for letting things go this far.

The backs of her fingers brushed his erection and his penis jumped in response.

Ross groaned, grabbed her hand, lifted it to his mouth and kissed the tips of her fingers. 'Not tonight, Ally.'

Ally stared at him, bemused. 'Why not?'

His knuckles rubbed her cheekbone. 'Because you still have that what-the-hell-am-I-doing? look in your eyes. When we come together—and we *will* come together— you're going to want this as much as I do and you'll have no regrets in the morning. Sorry about your panties.' Ross leaned forward, kissed her cheek and tapped her nose. 'Swing by with that offer on Monday before you leave.'

Ally perched on the desk with her legs firmly closed, watched him pick up the wallet and car key he'd left on the coffee table. It was only after the door snicked closed behind him that his words actually made sense.

They still had business to do. She'd have to pretend that he *hadn't* brought her to a stunning orgasm while she presented Bellechier's offer and—nearly as annoying—he'd destroyed one half of an expensive lingerie set.

But, my oh my, it had been so worth it.

Three steps forward, thirty back, Ross thought as he lifted his head up and saw Ally at his office door, a sheaf of papers in her hand. Her hair was pulled off her face, curls tamed into a tight knot at the back of her neck, and she wore a severe black skirt that ended just above her knee and perfectly applied make-up on that face that said, 'Let's pretend that you *didn't* see me orgasm around your fingers.'

That cool, remote, can't-mix-business-with-pleasure face.

They were two single healthy adults who were smart enough to recognise the line between the two...well, *he* was at least. He was beginning to realise that while Ally was a sharp operator in the boardroom, she was less experienced in the bedroom.

Why? She was smart, gorgeous, had a body made for sex… She should be a lot more at ease with the hot and heavy stuff than she had been on Saturday night. And he knew that it had been a long while since she'd had an orgasm like the one he'd given her.

'Hi,' Ally said, her hand on the frame of his door, her eyes wary.

'Hi, back. You're later than I expected,' he said, pushing back his chair and standing up behind his desk.

'Sorry. I thought that it was silly to come across town and then go back to the hotel, so I'm heading straight for the airport when I leave here.' Ally waved her hand. 'I have a taxi coming back for me in half an hour.'

Pic, realising that his latest crush was back, let out a deep, appreciative bark and lumbered to his feet, shoving his snout into Ally's free hand. Ally sent Ross a quick look, handed him the papers and bent over and rubbed his dog's head. Pic's eyes rolled back in his head and he moaned with pleasure.

Ross knew exactly how he felt.

He walked around his desk and sat on the corner, his legs stretched out in front of him. He flicked the papers with his thumb. 'So this is the offer?'

Ally straightened. 'Yep.'

'Will I be happy with it?' Ross asked.

'Why don't you take a look and see?' Ally retorted, sitting on the arm of one of his easy chairs and crossing her legs.

Ross couldn't help looking at that slim thigh under the black cotton and a picture of her legs falling open in front of him scorched his retina. He heard her panting, remembered how she'd looked without the covering of those silly panties…hot and wet and slick with pleasure.

He was instantly half hard, his dick protesting against his zip. That line between business and pleasure could blur with one memory, he realised with a shock. That hadn't happened before. *Friggin' hell.*

He stared at the distorted words in front of him as he attempted to get control of his raging hard-on, tried to keep from reaching for her and slamming his mouth against hers and pushing his way home. *This is what happens when you spend your days imagining taking her ten ways to Sunday,* he moaned to himself.

'So, what do you think?' Ally asked.

Ross looked at her, confused. 'About what?' *Taking you right here? Sure, let's go.*

Ally gave him a what-the-hell? look. 'The offer, Ross. Does it work for you?'

Oh, the offer. He was scrunching it in his hand. 'Let me read it again,' he said.

Hell, he needed to read it for the first time. Pulling in a deep breath, he skimmed through the Bellechier offer, didn't quite believe what he was reading and read it again.

'Holy hell, Jones, this is unbelievable.' They'd literally made him an offer he couldn't refuse. He wouldn't need to do any extra fundraising for the think tank for the next two years if he accepted their offer. He could buy a lot more equipment than he'd originally wanted, and could finance the research into so many more projects than he'd originally envisaged.

He just needed to give them his face and lend his name to their campaign for a limited period. It was a no-brainer...

'I could push them for more if you're not happy,' Ally said, erroneously interpreting his silence as displeasure.

Ross considered her words for a minute. The businessman in him was savvy. Her words suggested that they were prepared to go even higher. But the moralist in him said that they'd already offered nearly seven times more than he really wanted and he was grateful. He wouldn't push his luck.

'No, I'm good. This offer is fantastic.'

He saw the look of relief that flickered across Ally's face.

'You thought I'd push you for more?' he said, and caught her nod.

'Everyone does,' she replied. 'We pride ourselves on

making fair offers but people invariably want more. The negotiations become…'

She fell silent and Ross filled in the words for her, trying to help her identify the emotion, the word she was looking for. 'Annoying? Disheartening? Tedious?'

'Tedious.' Ally picked up the word, tasted it and then nodded her approval. 'Celebrities are…greedy. I'm glad you're not. If you sign both copies you can keep the top one and I'll take the other one back to Geneva.'

Ross stood up, reached for a black pen and placed the documents on his desk, signing his name where she indicated. 'What now?' he asked, handing her a copy.

'We send you a proper contract, you get your lawyers to look it over and you send it back to us. I get started on the fun stuff—designing the campaign, which includes both commercials and print ads.'

Ally tucked the papers into the side pocket of her bag and resumed her spot on the arm of the chair. Pic, the tart, placed his jowls on her thigh and looked adoringly up at her as her fingers disappeared into his coat.

Ally looked at her watch. 'My taxi will be here soon. I need to get going.'

He didn't want her to leave—not just yet—so he held up his hand to keep her in her seat. 'I do have a few provisos with regard to the campaign,' Ross stated, in his best non-negotiable tone of voice.

Ally tipped her head. 'Okay…what are they?'

'Everything I'm needed for has to be shot in Cape Town. I've still got a business to run here.'

Ally didn't reply at first, and he could almost see her gears turning.

'I'm sure we could make that work. It's a stunning city.'

'And I want *you* to oversee this project. You are here for every minute the camera crew and the photographers are here. If I'm involved then you're involved. It's your baby. You don't hand it off to one of your lackeys.'

By her immediate frown Ross knew that this would be

problematic—or that she would make it more problematic than it had to be. Ally... Hell, she could complicate jelly.

'I can certainly spend a day or two in Cape Town, but once the concept and storyboards are approved the rest of the project is in the hands of the ad agency.'

'I want you here,' he said stubbornly. Partly because he didn't like the idea of being passed off onto the ad agency, but mostly because he couldn't get his hands on her, get her out of his system, if she was on another damn continent.

'The rest of my work doesn't stop because you want me in Cape Town, Ross. And this will take a couple of weeks at least—it's going to be tricky for me to be away from the office for that long.'

'You can bring your laptop with you and nobody is indispensable. Delegate. Make it happen, Jones.' There was no room for discussion in Ross's voice.

'How much wiggle room do I have on this?' Ally asked.

'Absolutely none,' Ross replied. He folded his arms and stared her down. 'I thought that this project was a priority—that you had to make this happen no matter what else bounced onto your desk?'

'It is—you know it is,' Ally retorted. 'And I would, except that... Hell.'

She stared off into space and Ross waited, knowing that she would capitulate eventually. Not only because the campaign was important but also because she wanted to take last night's...experiment...to its logical conclusion.

'Okay, I'll temporarily move to Cape Town. Anything else?'

Ross wanted to suggest that she pick up five kilos before she returned, and tell her that he didn't want to see any raccoon rings around her eyes, but he thought that he might be inviting a slap.

'No.'

'I really have to go.'

Was that regret he heard in her voice or just wishful thinking? He wished he could tell.

'Yeah. I'm sorry I can't take you to the airport but I have a meeting in fifteen.' Ross held the door to his office open and waited for her to walk through. 'I'll walk you down.'

'Thank you.'

Why did his heart feel so heavy at the thought of her going? What was wrong with him? Women passed in and out of his life all the time and he never thought twice about it, but he felt hollow thinking that Ally was another of those passing ships. *Get a grip, Bennett. She'll be back in a few weeks.*

'What time is your flight?' Ross asked guiding her along the side of the downstairs offices—ignoring the speculating glances of his staff—to the front door.

'This afternoon,' Ally said, pulling her sunglasses out of her bag as they stepped into the hot sunshine.

The taxi was parked a couple of feet away, ready and waiting to take her away from him. Ross grabbed her elbow to hold her still and she slowly turned to look at him, tipping her head back to look into his face. 'It's been…interesting.'

Ally's sexy mouth quirked as she pushed her hair out of her eyes. 'That's one way of putting it.' She reached up and planted a kiss on his cheek, holding her face against his for a moment as if to soak in his smell. 'Bye, Ross.'

Ross touched her face again. 'Bye, Jones. See you in a couple of weeks, okay?'

Ally managed a small smile and they walked over to the taxi. Ross opened the back door and waited until she was inside before slamming it shut. The taxi pulled away and Ross watched it turn the corner and disappear out of sight.

Ross shoved his fist into his sternum, like Ally often did, and turned to go back into his building.

She was breathtaking, in a fist to the solar plexus kind of way. *Not good*, he thought. But he had a couple of weeks to wrap his head around that. Because he had no intention of letting her become important.

No intention at all.

CHAPTER SIX

ALLY LOOKED OUT of her window into the pouring rain and leaned back in her office chair. A few days ago she'd been swimming in the Indian Ocean and riding on the back of Ross's bike in the hot, hot African sunshine and she missed it.

She missed *him*. Which was ridiculous, since she hardly knew the guy. But the reality was that her life, never a carnival, had seemed a little more monochromatic since she'd returned from Cape Town, her mood a little bleaker. And, although she knew there was no point, she kept checking her e-mail to see if maybe—possibly—miraculously—an e-mail from him would pop into her inbox… Just a *Hello, how are you doing?* Anything to let her know that he was thinking of her as much as she was thinking of him.

She couldn't even find anything to e-mail him directly about—and she'd tried. Legal was dealing with the contracts, and nothing was settled yet with regard to the adverts themselves. The Bellechier stylist had e-mailed him to get his clothing and shoe sizes, so there was nothing she could use as an excuse to make contact.

Damn.

She was behaving like a teenager, wishing and projecting like this. Realistically she knew that Ross hadn't given her—Ally Jones, not the campaign—another thought since she'd left RBM in that taxi; why should he? He had a busy life that she wasn't a part of.

Ally cursed softly at the knock on her door and, seeing Sabine behind the glass panel next to the door, nodded for her to come in. She stood up and met her foster mother as she entered the room, kissing her on both cheeks and accepting a quick hug.

Sabine sat down and crossed her still lovely legs. 'I came to see if I can take you to lunch.'

Ally gestured to the piles of paper on her desk. 'I'd love to but I have so much to do.'

'You always do.' Sabine cocked her head. 'How are the arrangements coming along for the campaign?'

Ally wrinkled her nose. 'Fine. The ad company sent through their storyboards earlier and they are wonderful. Ross will be...*is*...utterly perfect... I mean they've done a good job.'

'"Utterly perfect"? That's an interesting choice of words.' Sabine's lips twitched.

Ally lifted her head at another knock on her door and her assistant shoved her head inside.

'Hey, Francine. What's up?' she asked in French.

'I have something for you.'

Ally gasped as she saw the huge bouquet of purple and blue flowers in Francine's arms.

Francine tottered over to her desk and handed her the card. 'Afrique du Sud.'

Ally resisted the urge to rip open the envelope, her heart thumping. There was only one person she knew in South Africa... Wow, this was better than any e-mail.

Sabine peered at the blooms as Ally took the bouquet from Francine, reverently touching the petals as if she'd never seen flowers before.

'Do you know what flowers they are?' she asked Sabine.

Sabine nodded and pointed. 'Blue orchids, anemones, hydrangeas, sweet peas, delphinium and Bachelor's Button. Dear Lord, it is beautiful. From whom, *ma petite*?'

Ally placed the card on the desk and handed the flowers back to Francine. 'Can you find a vase for me and bring them back?'

'Sure.' Francine took the bunch and hopped from foot to foot, hoping to hear the answer to Sabine's question.

Ally knew that if she exhibited the smallest bit of curiosity Francine would pepper her with questions. Her assistant had no concept of boundaries and tact. Then again, neither did Sabine.

'Thanks, Francine,' Ally told her assistant, and grinned at her obvious frustration.

Sabine just crossed her legs and looked inquisitive. Ally wouldn't be able to dismiss her as easily.

She sighed, knowing that Sabine would out-stubborn her. 'They are from Ross.'

'Ah…that's quite a gesture from someone you've just met.'

'I… He's…' Ally bit the inside of her lip and stared at her desk. She wished she was one of those women who could just open up, spill what she was thinking. She knew that Sabine wished she was too.

'Talk to me, darling. Please.'

Okay, maybe she could try. Just this once…

She presumed that Sabine knew that she wasn't a virgin, although she'd never brought a man home. Around the time that she'd felt she *could* take one home, they had all—to a man—dumped her because they were tired of playing second fiddle to her work.

Ally licked her lips. 'We had a very hot encounter…'

Sabine's thin eyebrows lifted. 'Sex?'

'No, just a hot kiss.' Well, that wasn't quite all, but she wasn't telling her that.

Sabine pouted in disappointment. '*Pfft!* You need sex, not a kiss…'

'Tante Sabine!'

Although, honestly, she couldn't disagree. She *did* need sex—now more than ever. A toy would never cut it now.

'Alyssa!' Sabine retorted. 'You need sex like nobody I've ever encountered. It's an amazing method of stress relief.' She examined her fingernails, her expression mischievous. 'Why do you think that Justin and I are so…how do you English say?…frigid?'

'Chilled,' Ally replied, before putting her hands over her ears. 'And I *so* didn't need to hear that.'

'Sex releases endorphins….'

'La-la-la-la.' Ally stuck her fingers in her ears. 'Heard of the expression *too much information*, Sabine?'

'Between friends? Mother and daughter? *Non!*' Sabine stood up, walked around the desk and placed her cool hands on either side of Ally's face. 'Darling girl, you need a man. You need sex. You need fun. You need not to work so hard. You need to let people in. You need to chill. And, *mon Dieu*, you need to eat!'

Ally covered those hands with hers. 'I know that you think you know best…'

Sabine's frown warned her to be careful.

'But I am fine—I really am. I'm busy and productive. I'm happy.'

Sabine removed her hands, but not before tapping Ally's nose with a red-tipped finger. 'This grew bigger with that lie, Alyssa.' She shook her head in frustration before walking across the room to the door. 'I'll order lunch to be sent up to you from the deli on the corner.'

Sabine needed to fuss and to nurture and Ally was happy to let her order lunch if it made her happy. 'Thanks, Tante Sabine, that would be great.'

'Any chance of showing me the card?' Sabine asked hopefully as she reached the door.

'No.'

'Zut!'

As soon as Sabine had closed the door behind her Ally reached for the card and ripped the envelope open. After much cursing—had they used superglue to seal the flap?—

she yanked the plain white card out of the envelope and flipped it open, her stomach quivering with anticipation.

He'd scanned his note and sent it to the florist, who'd pasted it onto the card. His handwriting was strong and masculine and untidy.

Blue… I'm noticing it a lot lately and not one shade matches your eyes. Maybe one of these flowers will.
Ross

Ally hiccupped a laugh and buried her face in the fragrant bouquet, her heart pounding a staccato beat. So he *was* thinking of her…had thought of her enough to make him order a bouquet of expensive blue flowers.

Her stomach was fizzing with pleasure—a very pleasant change from the scorching heat of heartburn.

It was a thoughtful, lovely, sexy gift and it deserved at the very least a response. His business card was attached to her stationery jar and on it was his personal e-mail address. It would be so easy to drop him a quick line…

Ally reached for her laptop and thought a while.

To: rossbennett@rbmedia.com
From: AJones@bellechier.com
Subject: Nice surprise.
I didn't realise that my eyes had made such an impression on you…
Ally.
PS The bouquet is stunning. Thank you so much.

It wasn't a minute before his reply appeared in her inbox.

To: AJones@bellechier.com
From: rossbennett@rbmedia.com
Subject: Re: Nice surprise.
Your eyes are amazing but your boobs, butt and legs are even better. You are the reason I toss and turn at night.

To: rossbennett@rbmedia.com
From: AJones@bellechier.com
Subject: Um...
Not sure what to say to that except that we did—do—
seem to have an unexplainable and hectic chemical re-
action.

My sleep has also been disrupted by certain memories...and fantasies.

The mouse hovered over the 'Send' button as she de-
bated whether to send it or not. What the hell? she thought,
but immediately wished she could pull it back as it winged
off. What was the point of exchanging flirty, sexy e-mails
with a man so far away? What could they do about it except
become increasingly frustrated?

To: AJones@bellechier.com
From: rossbennett@rbmedia.com
Subject: Re: Um...
Am about to go into a meeting and now have a hard-on.
Thanks a bunch.

When are you going to give me one I can actually use?
With you?

Holy frosting on a cupcake, Ally thought, and licked her
lips as moisture appeared between her legs.

Before she could formulate a reply—dear God in heaven,
what could she say to *that*?—another message appeared in
her inbox.

To: AJones@bellechier.com
From: rossbennett@rbmedia.com
Subject: Re: Re: Um...
Is that a possibility?
A straight-up, no-strings offer this time. All personal and
no business.

Was it? Ally thought quickly and thought hard. She was incredibly attracted to Ross, and he'd made her feel more alive than she'd felt in months…years. Maybe she needed to step out of the comfort zone she was in and live just a little.

They could have a brief, hot, fizzy affair when she went back to Cape Town. An affair that had a time limit—a logical conclusion. One that made her feel in control, secure, because it couldn't carry on for longer than that. He lived on another continent and there was no possibility of her getting emotionally attached because there wouldn't be enough time. Besides, she didn't open up to anybody and it wouldn't be any different with Ross…

It would be a working holiday, she thought; the best of both worlds. She'd work during the day, as she always did, and hook up with him at night.

What would be the harm? Having some fun… Everyone—okay, Sabine—was telling her to have some fun, some sex, so why not with him?

To: AJones@bellechier.com
From: rossbennett@rbmedia.com
Subject: Dying here…
You still there? Need a reply, Jones, or else I'm going to be less than useless in this long, long meeting…which is about to start!

To: rossbennett@rbmedia.com
From: AJones@bellechier.com
Subject: Re: Dying here…
When I get back to Cape Town, maybe. That'll not be for another four weeks, though…

And, just to be clear, we're talking a hook-up only, right? No messy emotions. No expectations. I don't do emotions and have no expectations.

To: AJones@bellechier.com
From: rossbennett@rbmedia.com
Subject: I'll make a plan.
I can't wait that long so I'll come to you. A hook-up works for me... I don't do long-term either.

Got to run...enjoy the flowers.
Later.

Ally stared at her screen and couldn't believe that she'd agreed to have sex with Ross. Had she lost her ever-lovin', cotton-pickin' mind? Was she bat-mad insane? She didn't do hook-ups, one-night stands, have crazy sex with men she hardly knew.

Then again, if she didn't do any and all of the above then why was she feeling so damn pleased with herself?

Ross was worse than useless for most of the meeting; thank God it was largely technical talk, which Eli could handle, allowing him to drift.

She'd said yes...
Friggin' hell.

He couldn't believe it. He'd thought that he'd lob it out there and had expected a snotty equivalent to a kick in the nuts rebuke.

Ross checked the e-mails on his mobile; nope, he hadn't been imagining the whole thing.

She'd agreed to a casual hook-up. *Hurrah.*

He hadn't been able to stop thinking about her... Her long legs, flat stomach, the deep blue of her eyes. The perfect feminine bits of her...

Okay, not a good time to go there... He slipped his hand under the table and adjusted himself to find a little comfort.

It had been a long, long time since a woman had had the ability to give him a hard-on just from a memory—to distract him like this, to creep under his mental skin. One minute he'd be concentrating on some paperwork and the next she'd leap into his head, like a mischievous kid who hid behind doors and yelled *boo*!

She was such an intriguing mix between business and sexy, smart and vulnerable. And wild… There was a lot of passion bubbling under the severe clothes and the strait-laced attitude. He wanted to be the one to release that passion…the one who held her while she was burning with it. The one who was inside her when she screamed from it, exploding around him.

That was if he didn't spontaneously combust from sheer frustration first.

He *had* to get to her.

Logistics, logistics… Ross tapped his mobile on the boardroom table. He wanted to go online and book the first flight out to Geneva, be there by late tonight. But that was crazy and would make him look desperate. What he should do was combine it with a trip to see his mother in London, his sister in York. He could interview that new computer animation student who was reputedly brilliant. After a little work he could pop over to Geneva late Thursday afternoon, take Ally to dinner and then to bed.

If it worked out the way he planned they could spend the weekend together before he needed to be back at Heathrow to catch a plane on Monday night—

Eli jabbed him in the ribs and Ross frowned at him. 'What?'

'Stop tapping that bloody mobile and concentrate!' Eli hissed.

Yeah, okay, Ross thought. But his mind immediately went sliding back to Ally. He was going halfway across the world to have sex. Was he mad? There were plenty of willing girls in Cape Town. But he didn't want them. He wanted her. He just didn't understand why. He had no idea as he certainly didn't want to be intrigued by an uptight workaholic whose life was her job.

She was the perfect hook-up—she had no expectations and didn't 'do' emotions. It was a good job he wasn't thinking of her in terms of anything more—like a lover or a partner—because then he'd be screwed. He just needed to get this woman out of his system. If he slept with her maybe he could banish her from his thoughts and dreams.

No, if he were looking for a lover then no way would he choose an uptight workaholic like his dad. Loving someone who was wedded to their job was a good way to get kicked in the teeth and to end up feeling lonely, unloved, emotionally and physically abandoned.

No, the minimum he expected from a lover was to come first, and that would never happen with Jones. And that was okay. This was only about making *her* come first anyway.

Ross grinned and Eli jabbed him in the ribs again. 'For God's sake, Bennett, get a grip and concentrate!'

Ross looked around at the faces of the people—some annoyed, some amused, all curious—and thought that maybe Eli was right.

He might not be corporate but he was normally professional.

'You still enjoying my flowers, Jones?'

Ross's deep voice slid across the miles and over her skin and Ally shivered. She automatically glanced at her watch and saw that it was past ten. It was still raining. Leaning back in her chair, she placed her feet on her desk—something she would never normally do, but since she was pretty sure she was the only one in the Bellechier building at this time of night she thought she could.

'They are looking a bit sad,' Ally admitted, looking at the drooping bunch on her desk. 'The orchids are still fine, so I'm going to take them home with me tonight.'

'You're still at work?'

Ross swore and she imagined him raking his hand through his hair.

'You need to get a life, woman.'

'Apparently I am—unless you've called me to rescind

your invitation,' Ally said. Her voice was cool although she sucked in shallow breaths.

'Not a chance. But why are you still at work?'

'Long day... Looking over sponsorship deals and the set-up for two new stores in Hong Kong and Miami. Brainstorming storyboards with the ad agency for your campaign.'

'Do *not* make me look like a wuss,' Ross threatened.

'Ah...there goes my idea of dressing you up in skintight shirts and pants and having you arranging flowers and composing haikus,' she teased.

Ross chuckled.

'Where are you?' Ally asked, needing to know.

'Standing on my veranda overlooking the Atlantic Ocean, listening to the sound of the waves crashing on the rocks. Drinking a glass of red wine.'

Ally closed her eyes. 'Damn, that sounds good.'

'Well, get your ass over here. I'll ply you with wine and do wicked things to you,' Ross suggested, his voice deep as night, rich as Swiss chocolate and so, so sexy.

Dear God, she was tempted. So tempted. But she couldn't; she had too much on the boil here—too many responsibilities, too much that could go wrong. She needed to make this job work, needed to make these projects a success...failure was not an option.

'I wish I could but it's simply not possible. Even the time I spent in Cape Town has put me days behind in my schedule.'

'Yet the world keeps turning,' Ross muttered. 'You're a workaholic, Jones.'

No, she wasn't. 'I'm just dedicated.'

'Trust me—I know one when I see one.'

Ally heard Ross take a sip of his wine and wondered why he sounded so bleak, so sad.

'Don't burn out, Jones.'

She frowned at his terse tone. 'I'm fine.' Dammit, she was saying that a lot lately.

Ross was quiet for a little while and Ally was happy to

listen to him breathe, to hear the occasional thud of a wave in the distance.

'How close are you to the beach?' she asked eventually.

'Not far. You walk out of my yard onto the dunes; the beach is just beyond that. Easy access—which is perfect since I surf most days.

'So...the reason for my call. I am going to be in London in two weeks' time. I have business on the Tuesday and Wednesday and thought I could fly to Geneva on the Thursday evening. Does that suit?'

Ally asked him to hold on while she consulted her diary. She knew that she was flying in from Hong Kong on the Wednesday. She'd have Thursday at the office to catch up, so she could probably skip out early that evening. Was she going to do this? Really?

She took a huge breath and jumped. 'That could work.'

'Good,' Ross said, his voice so low and so hot that it set her nerve-endings on fire, her pulse jumping and her panties damp. Dear God, if this was what he could do to her over the phone, then he'd be lethal in the bedroom. 'Two requests, okay?'

Oh, frig, what? Whips? Chains? Blindfolds?

Ally licked her lips. 'What?'

'Wear those red panties for me.'

'Okay. What else?' *Please let it not be anything weird... please.*

'Leave the office now. Eat something. Get some sleep.'

Okay, not what she was expecting. Ally looked at her monitor and the half-finished report on the screen.

'It'll still be there in the morning, Jones,' Ross said, reading her mind from miles and miles away. 'Drop your feet, push your chair back, grab your bag and go.'

Surprisingly, Ally found herself doing exactly what he'd said.

Her last thought as she drifted off to sleep—the first time in months and months that she was in bed before eleven—was that if he could get her to do his bidding over the phone, how much more difficult would it would be to refuse him anything face to face?

Ally pulled a pillow over her head and prayed that he wasn't into kinky sex. She just wasn't ready for anything like that...

Yet.

CHAPTER SEVEN

ALLY STOOD IN her bathroom in her one-bedroom, open-plan loft apartment in the heart of Geneva and realised that she was sweating.

Buckets.

Wiping her face with her facecloth, she looked at her sheet-white face in the mirror above the sink and blanched. Her face was green-tinged and her eyes were huge and round, red-rimmed. She wished she could blame it on jet lag—the flight back from Hong Kong had been diverted and delayed—but she flew first class, which wasn't exactly torture.

No, it was time to admit that she was getting sick…and within twelve hours Ross would be here.

Ross—here. And she was looking like something the dog had rolled in.

She'd be okay, she told herself, ignoring her pounding head. She was just stressed and on edge. Nothing that three layers of make-up and a bucket of aspirin couldn't fix.

Ally had thought that a fortnight would give her ample time to prepare for her night of—she fervently hoped—debauchery. Before she'd left for Hong Kong she'd dashed out of the office for a bikini wax, a pedicure and a full body scrub. Yet, despite her primping and preening, she was having second, third and sixteenth thoughts about what she was doing.

On one hand the idea of him flying in to see her made her

feel like the world's sexiest woman; on the other she was really worried about how she'd interact with him once they'd finished scorching the sheets. Would it be awkward? Weird? Should she ask him to leave straight away or would he stay the night? She had to be at work early on Friday morning for a meeting—would she leave him to sleep or wake him up and kick him out?

Dilemmas…dilemmas.

And, on top of it all, she'd started feeling…well, *blah* yesterday—light-headed and headachy. She'd initially put it down to not eating enough, and had ordered a chicken salad on the flight, but even after eating it she'd still felt sub-par.

Ally looked at the sweat beads on her forehead and shivered in her thick dressing gown.

She could no longer ignore the band of pain that encircled her stomach like the gnawing, heated teeth of a Tasmanian devil. She could practically trace the path of the pain—it felt like a red-hot wire under her skin. Unlike the heartburn, which came and went, this was relentless hell.

Ally gripped the basin as misery, wet and cold, encircled her heart. How was she supposed to be a sex goddess—even have sex—feeling as she did now? Looking like an extra in a zombie movie? As much as she wanted to sleep with Ross, what she *really* wanted to do was to crawl up into a ball and suck painkillers.

Ally straightened, pulled out her tongue at her reflection, opened her bathroom cabinet and rooted around for a bottle of painkillers. She shook a couple into her hand and swallowed them down with a half-glass of water. Bunking off work was not an option. Apart from her tryst with Ross later that day, she had a meeting with the creative director of her favourite ad agency to discuss the commercials for the new line and she had a directors' meeting that afternoon.

She'd be fine. She just had to get to work and get busy and she'd forget that she wasn't feeling well.

By midday Ally realised that she wouldn't be doing much for the rest of the day, never mind showing Ross her brand-new, orchid-blue Bellechier negligee. She was running a temperature and the pain in her stomach was almost debilitating. Getting from her office to the ground floor of her building without passing out would be a challenge, and she felt so ill that driving home was not an option.

She couldn't do Ross—ha-ha-ha—not today. After calling for a taxi, she looked at her watch and nodded grimly. It was just on noon—plenty of time for Ross to cancel his flight. It wasn't fair to make him fly all the way to Geneva for a date with Morticia from the Addams Family. This simply wasn't going to work…

The pain clenching her heart was the twin of the one biting her stomach. Sucking up her courage and picking up her mobile, she dialled Ross's mobile number and couldn't help feeling relieved when it went immediately to voicemail.

'Ross, this is Ally. Sorry, but I really am not well and I have to cancel tonight. So, so sorry, but I wouldn't be any fun. At all. I hope you get this message in time so that you can cancel your flight.'

Ally rested her mobile against her chest and, fighting dizziness, quickly sent Ross an e-mail in the same vein. Leaning back in her chair, she blinked back the tears in her eyes… Well, that was that. She'd just blown a fantastic night by getting sick. She couldn't even have casual mind-blowing sex without stuffing it up.

Typical.

Ross was, to put it very mildly, supremely irritated as he stood in front of Ally's apartment block, staring up at the half-arch windows on the first floor. He'd spent the day chasing his tail around London, had barely made his flight to Geneva and had only picked up his messages in the taxi that he'd caught at Geneva Airport.

She was too sick to see him? BS! She'd just changed her mind and didn't have the guts to tell him. It had probably finally dawned on her that sex with him wouldn't be clini-

cal, professional, quiet and calm, and she wasn't ready for
hot and wild. Down and dirty.

Well, he was here, and he wasn't going to tuck his tail between his legs and just leave because Miss Uptight wanted
him to. He wasn't one of her corporate lackeys that she
could boss around and dismiss at a whim, Ross thought as
he lifted his finger to hit her apartment's bell.

What if she ignored him? Wouldn't let him in? Well, he'd
break down the damn door if he had to.

Luckily for him the door swung open and a teenager
stepped out, bopping her head to the music blaring out from
the headphones perched over her head. Ross caught the front
door before it clicked shut and walked into the hallway. Ignoring the lift, he walked to a set of narrow stairs, hoping
to take the edge off his anger before he reached Ally's top-
floor apartment.

Sick, my ass, Ross thought at the top of the stairs. Four-
teen, sixteen…there was her door. She probably had some
work that had landed on her desk today and she needed to
complete, because if she didn't it would signal the arrival
of the Four Horsemen of the friggin' Apocalypse.

And if she wasn't home he'd bloody well wait for her.
He might even barge his way into Bellechier itself, he was
that angry. Ross pounded on the door and felt his temper
ratchet up at the resulting silence. He pounded again and
heard the creak of a door opening, the faint shuffle of feet.

'Who is it?'

There she was, Ross thought, stupidly relieved. 'Open
the door, Jones.'

'What the hell…? Ross?'

The door opened and Ross looked into a snow-white face
and pain-addled eyes. His irritation disappeared and was
swiftly replaced with concern.

'Crap, you *are* sick.'

Ally's hair was scraped back from her face and she wore
a loose pair of track pants and a baggy long-sleeved top that
hid her curves and draped over her braless, perky breasts.

'I said that I was sick! Didn't you believe me?'

'Sorry,' Ross said, stepping into the hallway and dropping his overnight bag to the floor. 'I thought it was an excuse. What's wrong with you?'

'Damned if I know,' Ally muttered, walking into her lounge and sinking onto the couch, immediately lying down and placing her head on the armrest. She pulled up a thin blanket. 'Headache, pain in and on my stomach, and a rash. And I am so damn cold.'

Ross narrowed his eyes as he shrugged off his coat and laid it over the back of a chair. The temperature in the flat was like summer in the Karoo, and he immediately stripped off the V-necked jersey that covered his white T-shirt. Better, he thought, moving to sit on the couch next to her hip. She looked clammy, and when he touched her forehead with the back of his hand even he, novice that he was at Florence Nightingale stuff, could tell that she was running a temperature.

'Where's the rash, Jones?'

'Stomach,' Ally mumbled, and kept a firm grip on the blanket.

He easily tugged it away from her and lifted her shirt. He swore when he saw the belt of angry blisters below her navel. They looked vicious and painful and Ally winced when he rested his fingers on her bare hip, far away from the sores.

'That sore?' he asked, quickly lifting his hand.

'My skin is super-sensitive,' Ally said, her voice and face miserable.

'Guess sex is out, then. Unless you're prepared to get creative…' Ross teased, as much for his sake as for hers as he picked up a strand of damp hair from her cheek and pushed it behind her ear.

'You have about as much chance of getting lucky with me as you have of knitting fog.' Ally closed her eyes. 'I'm really sorry for putting you out but—and I'm asking you nicely—can you go now?'

'Why?'

'I look like hell, I have something on my stomach that is probably going to kill me soon, or infect the entire human race, I've been sweating buckets so I probably stink, and this isn't how I wanted you to see me.' Ally sighed. 'I bought a negligee.'

'Really?' Ross stood up and pulled his mobile from the back pocket of his jeans. He logged onto the internet and searched for hospitals. 'What colour is it?'

'The most beautiful blue.'

'Damn, I would've liked to have seen that,' Ross responded. 'Deep blue is my new favourite colour. I'm calling a taxi; where's your bedroom?'

'If you're leaving why do you want to know where my bedroom is?' Ally asked, her voice croaky.

Nice to know that she hadn't lost all of her smarts, Ross thought.

'I'm not leaving—we are. I need to get you a coat and a pair of shoes. I'm taking you to the nearest emergency room.'

'No, you are not. I'll be fine. I just need to rest.'

'Stop being an idiot, Ally. You are burning up, you have a rash that looks dreadful, and you're going to an ER if I have to throw you over my shoulder and carry you downstairs.'

Ally told him what to do with himself and Ross grinned at her feistiness. 'Actually, I had planned to do that to *you*.'

'Funny man.' Ally sat up and immediately shoved her head between her thighs. 'Why don't you just go and I'll take myself to a doctor?'

'I'm not that gullible. You'll just lie down again and in a week your family will find your bloated corpse. If you think you look bad now, just think how you'll look then,' Ross stated on a teasing grin. 'Stop arguing, sweetheart, you're going to the hospital.'

'Dear God, if I had known you were this annoying I would never have agreed to sleep with you,' Ally muttered as he walked back into the hall and down the short passage.

'I'm not annoying—you're just stubborn,' Ross said when he came back, a pair of comfy slouch boots in his large hand. 'Get your feet in these, Jones.'

'I don't need to go to the ER. I'll call for an appointment with a doctor.'

'Alyssa.' He sighed. 'Do me a favour…please? Since I've travelled over twelve thousand kilometres to see you?' Ross used his best woe-is-me voice and guilt immediately swept across her pain-gripped face.

'What?'

It worked every time. It was such a girl trick, but he had no compunction in using manipulation to get his way quickly.

'Let's just get this done. Because it's going to happen with or without your cooperation.' Ross hauled her to her feet and guided her to the door. He shoved her arms into the coat he'd found hanging on a hook behind the door, not fastening it so that the material didn't rub against her blisters.

Ally's face turned mutinous. 'Your bedside manner sucks, Bennett.'

Ross's look was full of irony. 'That's because what I had planned for you involved being *in* your bed, not at its side.' He dropped a hard but brief kiss on her lips. 'Let's go, zombie-girl.'

Ally had to smile. 'Screw you,' she said, but this time there was no heat in her words.

'Again, those were my plans…'

'Shingles.'

Ally looked down at the dark head of the doctor who was peering at the rash on her stomach and thought that he had a nicer bedside manner than Ross. He was kind and patient and rather cute… She looked at Ross, who was standing with his back to the wall, scowling at his mobile. He had a right to scowl. He'd had his night of nookie screwed up by—what had he said?—shingles.

'What causes it?' Ally demanded.

'It's a viral infection; most of us have the virus in our system and it takes something to trigger the infection. Suppressed immunity, sickness, stress...'

'Ding, ding, ding,' Ross said, not lifting his head.

'Why are you still here?' she demanded rudely.

'Oh, hoping for a miraculous recovery of both your libido and your sunny disposition,' Ross said lazily. 'Oh, wait... you don't have a sunny disposition.'

The doctor laughed and Ally wanted to throw something at him. Ross—not the doctor.

'So, on a scale of one to ten, how stressed are you?' the doctor asked.

Ally tried not to squirm in her chair. Okay, the last two weeks had been crazy, and she could lay a huge part of that on Mr Too-Sexy-To-Breathe over there. If he'd just said yes to the campaign and then left her alone, then she wouldn't be going clucking mad.

'Well?' the doctor demanded.

'Four.' Well, maybe a seven or a nine, but she wasn't going to admit that!

'A hundred and four. Frig, woman, you are like the poster child for what corporate stress looks like. Thin, wired, sleep-deprived,' Ross commented.

'*He* has the stethoscope around his neck, not you!' Ally pointed out.

'Nevertheless, he's not wrong,' the doctor stated, and Ally turned her glare onto him.

Typical men, they always stuck together.

'Prolonged stress lowers the body's immunity, which allows the virus to reactivate.'

'What's the treatment?'

'A course of antiviral medication. Rest. No stress.'

'Rest,' Ross repeated. 'No stress.'

Ally really needed to throw something at him. Unfortunately there was nothing within reach. 'Bite. Me.'

The doctor laughed. 'Jeez, you two are fabulous entertainment value. How long have you been together?'

'We are *not* together,' Ally stated, pushing the words out between her teeth.

'She's just using me for sex.'

'That's it…get out! Go! Now! *Shoo!*' Ally shouted at him, goaded beyond all measure.

'I'd prefer that you are not alone tonight, Ms Jones. You are still dizzy, and if you fall and crack your head there could be some nasty consequences.'

'Well, I don't want *him*,' Ally said in a huffy voice. Mostly because this wasn't the way she'd envisaged her first date with Ross.

She should be scented and clean—sexy, even. Her hair wouldn't be greasy, her eyes would not be looking as if she'd been smoking dope for six days straight, and she wouldn't have a headache that threatened to roll her head off her neck.

Ross just rolled his eyes at the doctor and clicked his tongue against the roof of his mouth. He smiled at Ally, totally unfazed. When she was yelling at him she felt fractionally better—not quite so miserable and defeated. And he didn't seem to be taking her bitchiness personally; it was almost as if he knew that along with feeling so sick she also felt scared and vulnerable, and that arguing made her feel marginally better.

'Is there a friend I can call?' Ross asked.

'No.'

Ally dropped her head. How had she arrived at this point in her life where she didn't have a single girlfriend she could call in an emergency? She'd always thought that she'd have time for friends, lovers, fun when she finished her studies, got her next promotion, finished the next project…

Ross's eyes hardened. 'Someone is going home with you tonight, Alyssa. And I'm not idiot enough to trust you to make the arrangements. I'll call Luc and he can organise someone to look after you tonight.'

Oh, dammit, she didn't want him to go—not really—but she couldn't ask him to stay. That wasn't what he'd offered.

And she most certainly did *not* want her family knowing about this.

The little colour in Ally's face drained away. 'Oh, no, Ross, don't. Please? I don't want to worry them. Please don't call Luc. He'll just call Sabine and Justin, and they'll call Patric and Gina, and they'll all rush to my apartment and... Please don't. They are more than I can handle right now.'

They'd fuss and fret, and Sabine would lecture her on taking care of herself and working too hard. Justin would look at her with agonised eyes and she'd feel smothered and guilty.

'If you can just see me back to my apartment, then you can go home.'

'Did you hear me? I don't want you left alone tonight,' said Dr Dishy. 'I'll keep you in hospital if I have to.'

Dammit—rock and concrete wall. 'Sorry,' she muttered at Ross. 'It's not what you came here for.'

Ross looked at her for a long, long time before finally nodding his head. 'I'll stay at the apartment tonight,' he eventually told the doctor.

Ally let out a long, relieved sigh and bit her lip. 'Thanks. I owe you one.'

Ross arched an expressive eyebrow. 'One? Oh, I think we passed *one* a while ago.'

Ally tipped her head up and stared hard at the ceiling. After a minute she dropped her eyes to the doctor's very amused face. 'Maybe I should stay here tonight, because if he carries on like this shingles might be the least of my problems. I might brain him senseless,' she mused as she swung her legs off the bed and started to stand. 'Ooh, dizzy...'

Ross walked into the café a couple of blocks from Ally's apartment and slipped off his coat as he looked for an empty table in the early-morning rush. Seeing that one was being cleared next to the window, he walked over there and practically begged the waitress to bring him a cup of coffee.

Ally didn't drink coffee—a fact he'd found out after turning out practically every cupboard she had in search of the magic potion. How could she not drink coffee? he wondered. It was practically its own super food.

After the night he'd just had he might need it injected straight into his veins, he thought, sliding into the chair and looking across the street to Lake Geneva. Pretty, he thought. Even if it *was* colder than a witch's heart.

Ross grabbed his left shoulder with his right hand and held his elbow to try and stretch out the knots that had formed in his shoulders from laying his six-foot-three frame on a couch made for a pygmy. Last night had been possibly the most uncomfortable, most boring night of his life. He'd taken Ally home, got her into bed, heated up a cup of soup for her. Soon after she'd passed out—possibly from the antihistamine injection she'd received in her luscious butt earlier.

Ross, thinking that work would be the last thing on his mind, hadn't brought his computer, and Ally did not own a television. Who didn't have a TV in today's day and age? Oh, right—the same contrary woman who didn't drink coffee.

But Ross had found her e-reader and spent the next couple of hours flipping from one business book to another—all guaranteed to put a guy into a coma. Didn't the woman do *anything* for fun? Did she even know the meaning of the phrase 'light entertainment'?

Despite his frequent checking on her, she hadn't stirred for the rest of the night, and when he'd left the apartment a half-hour ago she'd still been conked out. Before he'd left he'd made a couple of calls, and he'd also lifted her shirt to check her rash—it still looked horrible, but as far as he'd been able to see there were no new blisters.

Ally would be fine, physically, in a couple of days. Mentally—well, that was anyone's guess.

The woman was a bona fide basket case…and he had this crazy impulse to help her and he wasn't sure why. He'd thought that he was coming here for uncomplicated sex, but something in her white face and large eyes had him wanting to help and, God help him, protect her.

Why? She was a modern woman who would rather eat glass than admit that she needed help. Maybe because she was a little lost and a lot alone—why didn't she have friends? A social life? Someone she could call in a scrape? She obviously loved her family but didn't want to rely on them, and he suspected that her life consisted of working too hard and trying damn hard to be brave.

And that was why he was in this café, about to make a decision that he would probably regret later. *C'est la vie*, as Jones would say in her impeccable French.

Ross had just finished his second cup of espresso and was feeling a lot more human when Luc walked through the door of the café, looked around and immediately spotted him. Dressed in a grey suit and a raspberry tie, he looked every inch the corporate CEO Ross tried very hard *not* to be.

Ross stood up, shook hands and eyed Ally's foster brother as he ordered an espresso and a full breakfast.

When the waitress had left Luc leaned back, unbuttoned his suit jacket and looked at Ross with friendly but wary grey eyes. 'This is a surprise, Ross. What can I do for you?'

Ross thought that there was no point in beating around the bush. 'Your sister is at home, on her own, suffering from a nasty case of shingles.' He saw Luc's eyes harden, saw the obvious question in them. *How the hell do you know that?* 'We were going to have dinner last night but she fell ill. I took her to the ER and she's not well.'

Luc slumped down in his chair. 'And she didn't want you to tell us?'

'No. And I would've kept my word but I have to return to London. I have a computer game designer who is debating whether to move from his mother's house to Cape Town and he needs his hand held. Unfortunately he's brilliant, or else I wouldn't bother. I just don't think Ally should be on her own.'

Luc tapped his fingers on the wooden table, his grey eyes unreadable. 'Alyssa is very good at shutting us out.'

'Why?'

Luc's mouth turned grim. 'She'd have to tell you that. All I can tell you is that she is complicated. A little messed up.'

He knew that, Ross thought, yet it hadn't put him off. He raked his fingers through his hair, wishing he could tell Luc that he was worried she was on the fast track to a loony bin. That he wanted to see the shadows lift from her eyes…that he wanted her to relax and have some fun. But when Luc would ask why he was doing this for a woman he'd only met a couple of times and he wouldn't be able to answer.

Mostly because he didn't have a freaking clue. It wasn't as if he thought they were going anywhere, that they had a future. They just had—what had Ally called it?—a hectic chemical reaction.

'Does Ally know that you're here, telling me that she is sick?' Luc asked.

'No, she was still sleeping when I left. I need to get back to London and I can't wait for her to wake up. And her mobile is off.'

Her mobile was off because he'd removed the battery to said mobile and hidden it. He was really hoping that she would be sensible and stay in bed for the rest of the day, preferably the weekend. But he couldn't stay around to babysit her; he had things to do, a business to run.

And he had to be the Bellechier face.

Frick. He still hadn't wrapped his head around that either. He wasn't a 'face' type of guy. He was going to take a truckload of BS from his mates at the gym, his fellow surfers, his colleagues for this—everyone who friggin' knew him.

Ally *so* owed him.

Luc lifted his coffee cup in a Gallic toast as the waitress placed his food in front of him. 'She is not going to be happy that you told me. I thank you, but she won't.'

'I can handle Ally,' Ross stated and wondered if he actually could.

* * *

'You sicced my family on me? Thanks so much!' Ally said as soon as Ross answered her call. 'Why?'

'I'm busy. I'll call you back in ten,' Ross retorted.

Ally pulled out her tongue at her dead mobile and tossed it onto her desk, walking to her window and looking at the cloud-covered Alps in the distance. It was Tuesday morning and she was back at work, considerably better but not one hundred per cent. Her rash had subsided and the blisters had started to scab—*yuck*—and the headache was at a manageable level.

She'd woken up on Friday at eleven to an empty-of-Ross apartment. He'd left her a note

Fridge has food in it. Eat something! Rest. DO NOT GO TO WORK. I called and told your secretary you were taking a personal day. Implied that I was keeping you in bed...not sure if she believed me. We'll talk.

She'd still been feeling so dreadful that she hadn't had the energy to deal with his high-handedness so she'd just turned around, hopped straight back into bed and slept for the rest of the day.

She'd dealt with her entire family trooping in to see if she was alive on Saturday night, and after Sabine had shooed them out she'd gone back to sleep and slept all night. And most of Sunday.

Every time she'd woken up Sabine had been there, with a cool hand, or soup, or a facecloth. It had felt nice and comforting, and that had been scary, so she'd insisted that Sabine went home to Justin on Sunday evening. Sabine had gone, taking her hurt feelings with her. That was why she didn't want her around; Sabine wanted to fuss and fidget and Ally wanted to be alone. She knew how to take care of herself...

She'd started off her morning by searching her apartment for the battery to her mobile—finding it eventually in her coat pocket behind her door. There had been a dozen calls to return, more explanations to make, worried family to reassure.

Ally tapped her foot, impatient. Three more minutes—could she wait that long? She leaned her shoulder onto the wooden frame and rested her head on the glass. Their date had been an unmitigated disaster and yet Ross had never once showed his irritation or annoyance. Yeah, he'd needled her at the hospital, but she knew that he'd just been teasing. His laughing eyes and amused mouth had given him away.

He somehow knew that she found sympathy and coddling more difficult to deal with than mockery. She so appreciated that. And she appreciated him leaving, letting her get on with being sick and then getting better. She was also very grateful for the food in her fridge—not that she'd eaten much of it. It was the thought that counted.

Twelve minutes had passed and he still hadn't called back. At fifteen minutes she dialled his number again.

'Bloody Nora, Jones, give me break,' he groaned.

'I need you to talk to me. Now,' Ally said, not realising how breathy her voice sounded.

'Hold on.' Ally heard Ross asking for a twenty-minute break and heard the scrape of chairs, footsteps fading away. 'You there, Jones?'

'Why did you do it?' Ally demanded. A part of her—a small, wishful part—wanted to believe that he'd done it for her. The rest of her scoffed at the notion.

'Hello to you too. How are you feeling? Blisters gone?' Ross said, his tone pointed.

Ally sucked down her impatience. 'Better. Thanks for the food. And for taking me to the hospital. I'm sorry I messed up your evening. That you flew in for nothing.'

She could almost see Ross's shrug. 'No worries.'

Ally couldn't help noticing that he didn't say anything

like *There'll be another time*, or *We'll reschedule*. Maybe
he had cut his losses and was thanking God for his narrow
escape. She rapidly blinked away the moisture in her eyes.
Stupid to feel upset—it was just sex. Something she kept
telling herself that she didn't need and could live without.

'Why did you tell my family when I specifically asked
you not to?'

Ross was silent for a minute. 'I have no bloody idea.
Maybe I just thought that nobody should be that sick and
have to deal with it on their own—especially when they
have a family eager and willing to help.'

What was she supposed to say to that? 'I don't need help.'

'That's stupid. Everyone needs help now and again. Even
you, Wonder Woman.' Ross's heavy sigh passed over the
miles between them. 'I can't get back to Geneva, so when
can I expect you in Cape Town?'

'For the campaign?'

'I couldn't give a frig about the campaign. I'm thinking
about burning up the sheets with you.'

Ally hauled in a sharp breath as pleasure spiked through
her. She twisted a strand of hair around her finger. 'You still
want to sleep with me?'

'Did you think that me seeing you as Death Girl would
put me off?'

'Sort of.'

'I'm not that shallow, Jones.'

Before Ally's frazzled brain could formulate a reply, she
heard voices in the background and then Ross spoke again.

'I've got to get some work done. We'll talk later, okay?'

Oh, they'd talk again—he could be very sure of that. And
she'd tell him all that she hadn't managed to say earlier: that
she didn't approve of him interfering in her life and calling
her family, that they were about sex and little else and that
he couldn't do it again.

Her mobile beeped and Ally picked it up, her heart accelerating when she saw a message from Ross on her screen.

Okay, I know I went against your wishes but I couldn't stick around and I was worried about you. I don't particularly like worrying about you and I want it to stop. It's interfering with the X-rated fantasies I'm having about you. So help me to stop worrying about you. Eat. Sleep. Please?

Ally, her irritation replaced with confusion, typed a short message back.

I'll try.

Two days later...

To: AJones@bellechier.com
From: rossbennett@rbmedia.com
Subject: Important question...
I have something important to ask you...

To: rossbennett@rbmedia.com
From: AJones@bellechier.com
Subject: Re: Important question
That sounds ominous. But okay...

To: AJones@bellechier.com
From: rossbennett@rbmedia.com
Subject: Here it is...
What colour panties are you wearing today?

To: rossbennett@rbmedia.com
From: AJones@bellechier.com
Subject: RE: Here it is...
Dammit, Ross, I just spewed coffee over my keyboard!

Three days after that...

To: AJones@bellechier.com
From: rossbennett@rbmedia.com
Subject: Long conversation
That was a very long and detailed conversation about the campaign and the contract, Miss Jones. So glad we got so many points cleared up.

To: rossbennett@rbmedia.com
From: AJones@bellechier.com
Subject: Re: Long conversation
I got the impression that you were distracted. Got a lot on your mind?

To: AJones@bellechier.com
From: rossbennett@rbmedia.com
Subject: Yeah...doing you
Mostly I was just thinking that I'd prefer to hear different phrases falling from your lips...
Like... 'I love having your body on top of mine. It feels amazing.' Or... 'Faster! Faster!'

A week after that message...

To: rossbennett@rbmedia.com
From: AJones@bellechier.com
Subject: Torturing me
Ross, you're torturing me with the sexy messages. I don't know if I can do another week in this state of...

To: AJones@bellechier.com
From: rossbennett@rbmedia.com
Subject: Misery loves company

Frustration? Horniness? Well, get your ass over here and we can do something about it. Sick of flying solo. Getting RSI in my hand. :)

CHAPTER EIGHT

ONE INTERMINABLY LONG week later Ally, dressed in a soft white cotton dress that perfectly suited a balmy spring day in Cape Town, walked into the craziness of RBM's open-plan office and looked around for Ross. She lifted her eyes to the second floor and the glass-fronted offices and couldn't see him in his office or in the boardroom.

Since there wasn't a receptionist in sight, she grabbed the arm of a young man walking past and asked him where Ross was. He muttered something intelligible and pointed across the room.

Ross stood bent over the shoulder of the pink-haired woman and the potbellied pig was resting its snout on his foot. Ally stared at his broad back for a long time. She was here finally and she wasn't quite sure what to say to the man who'd spent the last couple of weeks telling her exactly what he intended doing to her as soon as he got her alone.

It had been four weeks of sexy, naughty foreplay and she was done with talking...

The saliva in her mouth dried as he stood up, turned around and noticed her standing there. Could he see that her heart was in her mouth? That her blood was pounding a beat between her thighs? Could he tell that she didn't want to wait one more day, one more minute, before knowing what he felt like, smelt like, how he tasted?

He'd kept her on a low simmer for weeks and she was

about to go off her head if he didn't do something about it...*immediately*.

Ross moved across the room towards her and when he was close enough, grabbed her hand and pulled her back through the front doors of RBM.

He lifted his hands and held her face. 'You're here.'

Ally nodded her head. 'Yep.'

'I thought you were coming in on Monday.' Ross ran his thumb over her bottom lip.

'Changed my flight. Is that a problem?'

'Not from where I'm standing.' Ross's eyes were as golden as the hot sunshine falling on her bare shoulders. 'I want to kiss you, but if I start I won't stop.'

He dropped his hands to her shoulders and ran his hands up and down her arms. Ally placed her hands on his chest, felt his rapid heartbeat under her fingers.

'You look great. Not zombie-like at all.' Ross linked his hands in hers and looked at her intensely.

She was surprised to see his Adam's apple bob, as if he were nervous.

'If I asked you to come with me, would you? Right now?'

'That depends. If you're taking me to bed, yes. If you're taking me away to make me eat, then no.'

Ross smiled and pulled her towards the parking lot. 'Bed first. Food later.'

'Deal,' Ally replied, taking the helmet he held out to her. She cradled it against her chest and moved to stand next to Ross, who'd already straddled his bike. She linked her hands around his neck and stared at his mouth. 'I really don't think I can wait for that kiss, Bennett.'

Ross took her helmet back, hung it over the handlebar and placed his helmet next to hers. Swinging his leg off the bike, he placed his hands on her hips and pulled her up and into him. Her stomach brushed his huge erection and her rock-hard nipples dug into his chest. The friction of cloth and heat and male hardness sent a rush of moisture between her legs.

Yet Ross still didn't kiss her. His mouth hovered above hers, waiting, teasing, delaying…

She couldn't take this any more, Ally thought, and launched herself upwards, slamming her mouth against his, desperate to taste him, inhale him. Her tongue slid over his lips, brushed his teeth and found his, and they indulged in a long, hot, sexy slide. She felt Ross's hands clench on her hips, the tips of his fingers kneading her skin. His body was filled with tension, bottled-up frustration, and she wanted to feel it shatter around her—because of her. Ally tipped her head so that Ross could plunder her mouth, lose himself in her as she wanted to do with him.

Instead he pulled back and closed his eyes.

'Why did you stop?' she whispered, confused.

'As I said, if I start I won't stop. And that would give *that* lot more than they bargained for.'

'Who? What?' Ally asked, dimly aware of a lot of whistles and cat-calling coming from a distance.

Ross shuffled her around, lifted his hand and gestured behind him with his outstretched thumb. 'Them.'

Ally looked over Ross's shoulder to the first floor of RBM, where a clump of Ross's staff, led by the pink-haired woman, were watching them with avid interest.

'Go, boss!' shouted Kate of the Pink Hair, and let out a loud whistle, pumping her fist in the air.

'Dear God…' Ally muttered.

'Find a room, kids!' she shouted.

Ally bit her lip and met Ross's laughing eyes. 'Why don't we do exactly that?'

Ross stepped away from her, picked up her helmet and lobbed it at her. 'I like the way you think, Jones.'

Ally had barely stepped through his front door when Ross grabbed her, wrapped one arm around her waist and used his other hand to tip her head up so that her mouth was at the perfect angle to receive his kiss.

He finally had her alone and he could loosen his grip on

his self-control. From the moment he'd seen her standing in RBM—hell, for the past five weeks—he'd wanted this, needed her like this. He wasn't holding back now and his hard, possessive kiss would tell her that he was a frustrated man who had the woman of his latest dreams in his arms and that he intended making damn sure that by the end of their lovemaking she would have forgotten her own name.

Ross kicked the door shut with his foot, turned her and walked her backwards so that her back was against the door, his chest flat against hers. Wanting to slow them down a bit—he was about to come in his pants as it was—he placed his hands on either side of her head and gentled his kiss, dialling down hot and wild to slow and sexy.

Ally whimpered in his mouth as she brushed her breasts against his chest, reminding him of exactly how turned on she really was. He lifted his head for a minute and stared down at her. Her cheeks were flushed with passion, her lips wet from his tongue, her eyes unfocused and wild.

He'd never felt this on edge, this crazy before. This woman was dangerous, he realised. She could slip under his skin, make him feel things he didn't intend to feel... He had to remind himself that this was only about sex.

She wasn't his type anyway. Obsessed, driven, vulnerable...

Ross couldn't help licking her lip before he forced himself to speak. 'Remember our deal, Jones?'

Ally's hands snuck under his T-shirt and he sucked in his breath as her hands danced across his stomach.

'Which one?'

'This is still only a hook-up, right? No emotions, no expectations.'

'Hell, yes. I don't have time for a man or a relationship,' Ally said, pushing his shirt up his chest, urging him to take it off.

Ross gripped the fabric behind his neck and pulled it over his head, dropping it to the floor. She immediately buried her face in his sternum, her tongue darting out to touch his skin. Ross groaned and shoved his fingers into her hair.

'You're not going mushy on me, are you?' Ally suddenly demanded, lifting her head.

'God, no!'

Ally licked one of his flat nipples and he shuddered. 'Why would you think I'm getting mushy?' he asked.

Ally lifted her head and looked him dead in the eye with passion-filled eyes. 'Oh, just all the concern about me eating and sleeping. I wondered...'

He had to watch that. 'I was just making sure that you had enough energy to keep up with me.'

'Ooh, I'm *so* scared.'

'You should be,' Ross told her, finding the zip at the back of her dress and sliding it down. He pulled the dress off her shoulders and it landed in a white puddle on his slate floor, and there she stood, in pure white lacy underwear. The fabric was so sheer that he could see her pink nipples, the strip of blonde hair between her legs.

Ross pulled her bra cup aside and dipped his head, taking her peaked nipple into his mouth. Ally arched her back, slapped her hand on the back of his head to keep him there as he stroked and laved her.

'Take it off...' Ally muttered, trying to put her hands behind her back to take her bra off.

Ross reached behind her, flicked open the clasp, and Ally pulled the material off and tossed it away. She wiggled out of her panties and stood in front of him, one leg slightly bent so that he could see the moisture on her feminine lips.

'Please touch me,' she whimpered. 'I need you to.'

Ross slid his finger between her legs, sighing at her wet heat. His thumb found her clitoris and she bucked as he touched her intimately, knowingly.

'I need you to touch me too,' he muttered against her mouth, before sliding his tongue into her mouth and his finger into her passage.

Ally yelped into his mouth. Down below she clenched around his finger, and he smiled at her reaction. *Oh, yeah, there was passion underneath.* So much wild passion. 'Now you touch me, Alyssa.'

He helped her, one-handed, to undo the button on his cargo shorts, waited impatiently as she slowly slid the zipper down. One small push had his pants around his ankles, but his erection was still constrained by his underwear, threatening to jump out. Ross flicked her clit with his thumb and another finger entered her.

Ally moaned.

'Just think how good it's going to feel when I am inside you.' Ross spoke in her ear. 'Dammit, Jones, stop playing around and get me in your hand.'

Ally ran a finger up his length and Ross was certain that he'd never been this hard, this crazy for a woman's touch. Her thumb brushed over that pulsing vein and the sensitive spot just below the head. He felt her wipe away drops of moisture and wished he was in her mouth and inside her channel, both at the same time.

He couldn't wait much longer to have one or the other happen.

Ross pulled out of her, stepped back and whirled away to reach for the wallet that he'd tossed onto the hall table earlier. He pulled out a condom and ripped the foil packet open with his teeth. He quickly sheathed himself and, keeping his distance from Ally, lifted his eyebrows.

'Door or bed?'

'Door, then bed,' Ally replied, her eyes on his erection.

She licked her lips and, seeing that pink tongue, he felt the last vestiges of his control fly out of the window. Grabbing both her wrists with one hand, he lifted her arms and held them above her head, which lifted her breasts up to his mouth. He pulled one peak into his mouth and then the other, shoving his hand between her legs. As Ally whimpered, moaned, begged above his head, he licked his way over her navel, bit her hipbone and finally settled on the honeypot between her legs. As his mouth took the place of his hand Ally bucked and yelled. One stab of his tongue, then another, and he tasted her excitement on his tongue.

'Oh, no, you don't. You're gonna come with me, Jones.' Ross pulled himself up, jammed his hands under her thighs and in one fast movement buried himself in her.

She felt so wondrous, so damned perfect, that he stopped pumping, just wanting to capture the perfection of feeling her for the first time. Awed at being allowed to share the wild, primal side of this fascinating woman.

Ally's head whipped from side to side. '*Nooooo.* Don't stop.' She pumped her hips, half pulled herself off him and then slammed down on him again.

Ross, entranced with seeing his Miss Uptight totally unhinged—for *him*—allowed her to ride him. He could feel her tension, hear her words begging for release, and he took control. Holding her against the wall, he pushed as far into her as he could and bucked his hips. Ally buried her face in his neck and took what he gave her, begging for more. When he was certain that he no longer had a smidgeon of control left he felt her shudder, felt her reach up to touch his penis, and he lost it, pumping wildly into her, desperate to follow her over that beautiful edge.

His orgasm exploded from him, rocketed up his spine and blew off his head. He groaned and cursed and shuddered as he tumbled over, Ally's hair in his mouth, her scent in his nostrils.

Eventually his heart slowed, his vision cleared and he realised that his arms and legs were straining under Ally's dead weight. She was slumped against him, her breath uneven. Ross pulled a strand of her hair out of his mouth and ran his hand over her bottom.

'You still alive, Jones?'

'Mmm…' Ally slid down his legs and leaned against him, relying on him to take her weight. '*Je suis heureux comme un poisson dans l'eau.*'

Ross leaned her against the wall and stepped into the

tiny toilet next to the stairs to rid himself of his soiled condom. Finally a reason for that stupid room made for gnomes.

'Say again?' he asked.

'Fish…water…happy as…' Ally looked down at her naked body and shrugged. 'Of course I'm still waiting for the feeling to come back into certain parts of my body.'

Ross stepped back into the room and grinned at her lazy eyes, her tousled hair. It was the most relaxed he'd ever seen her and he liked it.

And he'd loved the sex. So much so that he planned on doing it again. Very, very soon.

He walked over to Ally, held her fine jaw in his hand and kissed her gently, his tongue sliding into her mouth. She tasted like excitement and need and he felt himself rise to the occasion. Ally's hand reached down between them and her hot hand encircled his shaft. He went instantly, surprisingly hard.

It seemed that 'very, very soon' would be now. He could live with that.

'Bed?' Ally whispered against his mouth.

'Lead the way. I am, literally, in your hands.'

Later—a lot later—Ally lifted Ross's hand off her bare bottom and peered at the expensive watch on his wrist. A quarter to six. In the evening. Jeez, Louise.

Sighing with regret, she slid her leg up as her hand drifted over his flat stomach.

'Jones…' he groaned, and his eyes remained closed. 'I honestly can't. Hell, we haven't moved from this bed since lunchtime.'

Ally moaned as his thumb rasped her nipple. 'Can't handle it, huh? Simply no stamina!'

Within a second Ross had rolled her onto her back and was laughing down at her. 'Lack of stamina, my ass.'

'You have a very nice ass, but I'll save you from proving it because I have to get back to my hotel. I still have work to do tonight.'

Ross lifted an unimpressed eyebrow. 'It's nearly six, Jones. Most people are about to call it quits for the day or already have.'

'Most people didn't waste the entire afternoon having sex.'

Ross placed a hand on his heart and looked wounded. 'Waste? That's harsh. An afternoon having sex is never wasted. In fact I think it's a damn good use of one's time. Half the population of the world would agree with me.'

'The male half,' Ally replied. 'Before your ego drops to the floor and starts crying, I'll admit that it was the best time I've ever wasted.'

'Nice save. Where are you staying?' Ross asked, his hand exploring the curve of her butt. 'Not the Riebeek? That's on the other side of the mountain in Hout Bay.'

'Just for tonight.' Ally pushed at his shoulders and Ross moved off her. 'Luc has a friend who owns a flat in Camps Bay. I'm staying there for the next couple of weeks. I'll pick up the keys tomorrow and move in.'

'Camps Bay, huh? We're practically neighbours. This is Bantry Bay, then there's Clifton, then Camps Bay. Straight down Chappies.'

'Chappies?'

'Chapman's Peak Drive. As I said—a perfect commute.'

A perfect commute for a booty call.

Why did she feel irritated by the words that she knew he thought but didn't speak? Ally asked herself as she walked into his large en-suite bathroom, carrying her very crumpled dress and underwear in her hand. Sex, a booty call, a pleasure run…whatever they wanted to call it, it was exactly what they were indulging in, what they'd agreed to, what she wanted.

Wasn't it?

Ally splashed some cold water over her face in an effort to wake up her dozy brain cells. Of course it was… She was having a no-strings affair with a man who seemed to enjoy her and her body—a lot! He was successful, good-looking, had a rockin' body and knew what he was doing in bed.

It was all good. She wasn't here for conversation or cuddling. She was here primarily to get this campaign filmed and wrapped up, and 'doing' Ross was just a very nice side benefit.

Don't confuse good sex with affection, Jones. You don't have the time, the energy or the inclination for a relationship. You stand on the outside and look in...that's what you do...it's your thing.

Ross pounded his fist on the closed bathroom door. 'Hey, it looks like it might be quite a sunset. Do you want to take a walk to the beach and watch the sun go down? We could take a bottle of red and some glasses. I'll drive you back to your hotel afterwards.'

A sunset, red wine and a good-looking man? People got to know each other over red wine and sunsets; confessions were made and secrets were revealed. Ally, knowing that she was more susceptible than most to the ambience—having never been romanced in her life—knew that she had to refuse. She simply couldn't trust herself to keep her distance.

And whose fault is it that you've never been romanced? Ally heard Sabine's spiky voice in her head. *Yours, you imbecile! You've never allowed anyone to romance you—never opened yourself up enough to be romanced.*

Ally tossed back her head, put a polite smile on her face and opened the door. She managed to send Ross an impersonal smile. 'Thanks, but no. I think I should get going. I'm kind of tired.'

Ross, who'd pulled on a pair of jeans, nodded once before reaching for a shirt. Muttering a curse, he walked over to her, lifted her chin and kissed her nose. 'You are the most stubborn, contrary woman I've ever met. Just because we've had sex it doesn't mean that we can't be friends, Ally.'

Ally pulled her bottom lip between her teeth. She stared at the black and white photograph of sand dunes on the wall behind his shoulder. 'I think it's just…better—safer—if we don't.'

Ross looked at her for a long minute and Ally tried not to flinch under his scrutiny. Eventually he dropped his head in a curt nod and gestured her to walk out of the room first. 'I'll take you back to your hotel now.'

'Thank you.'

Ross drove her in his Jeep, leaving the top off so that the balmy spring air could blow through their hair. He loved Cape Town in spring, with the smell of the jasmine creeper that covered the wall at the bottom of his property filling the air with its sweet scent. His neighbours were starting to barbecue again after the cold, wet winter, and the lawns and gardens were lush and verdant. Spring was flower season in the Western Cape, and soon the countryside would erupt in colour.

He hoped that Ally stopped working long enough to take it all in. To appreciate the beauty. To stop and literally smell the flowers.

Ross thought that a drive along Chapman's Peak Drive at sunset was nearly as good as sitting on the beach watching the sun going down. The road was magnificent, and it was his favourite route to drive his Ducati. He stole a glance at Ally, who was looking down the sheer drop to the sea below, switching her gaze between the sea and the mountains looming above them. Ross kept one hand on the wheel of the car, easily negotiating the twists and turns in the road as the orange sun tossed sunbeams like petals on the green-blue-aqua-purple sea.

Ross pushed a button on the steering wheel and flipped through a playlist until Macy Gray's husky voice drifted over them. They didn't need to talk, Ross thought, but he'd like to. He wouldn't mind knowing what drove her incessant need to work—why she found it so difficult to make friends, be a friend, and why, when she'd been sick in Geneva, she wouldn't ask her family for help.

She was a tightly wound ball of contradictions, he thought, his finger tapping to the beat against the edge of the steering wheel. Wild, passionate, giving with her body, but the exact opposite with her mind. He'd meant what he said about being friends—he'd always managed to be and stay friends with his previous lovers, and friendship added an element of fun to sex…a lightness that stopped it from being mechanical.

Sex with Ally had been anything but mechanical, Ross admitted, conscious of the party still wanting to happen in his pants. It had been a long time since he'd had sex that was that explosive. And once hadn't been enough. He'd reached for her again and again and she'd responded, each time getting bolder and braver.

He really had to fight the temptation to turn the car around and take her back to bed.

Ally thought that she was emotionally self-sufficient, but he'd never seen anyone more in need of a mate—someone to make her take a deep breath, drink some wine on a beach at sunset, make her look at the flowers.

He'd be that mate—he was good at it—and when they weren't being friends he'd shag her senseless because he was good at that too. He wouldn't become attached—what was the point?—and he would make sure that she didn't either.

Ross pulled up in front of the imposing entrance of The Riebeek and a red-liveried doorman stepped forward to open her door. Before she undid her seatbelt Ross grabbed the back of her neck and gently pulled her head so that he could look into her face.

'I had a great afternoon.'

Ally darted a look at the doorman, blushed, and Ross shook his head. If the man hadn't already realised that they'd spent the afternoon in bed, Ally's blush and embarrassment flashed it in six-foot-high neon. The doorman, to his credit, kept his face impassive. Good man.

Ally pulled her seatbelt off and reached for the bag that she'd placed at her feet. She shoved her hand into her wind-blown, messy hair and pushed it off her face. 'It'll take a week or so before we have everything in place for the campaign.'

'Why so long?' Ross asked, unhappily reminded that he'd committed himself to being on the wrong side of a camera for the Bellechier campaign.

'The creative director and I need to scout locations, hire extras, models, et cetera. I have to get the collection you're wearing out of Customs. Things to do…busy, busy.' Ally pulled her bag over her shoulder. 'I'll try and give you a date for when we need you as soon as possible.'

Ally climbed out of the Jeep and stood there, looking a little nonplussed and trying hard to be businesslike. Not so easy when they both knew that he'd had his head between her thighs just hours before.

Ally tapped the edge of the door. 'I'll see you.'

'Yeah, you will.' Ross looked at her mouth before his eyes clashed with hers. 'Sooner than you think.'

And he'd make damn sure that it was a lot sooner than she felt comfortable with. Jones, he decided as he drove off, needed to be kept off balance to keep that busy mind of hers from thinking too much.

CHAPTER NINE

ROSS WALKED OUT of his front door and watched Ally climb out of the small car she'd hired for while she was in Cape Town, her hair pulled back and her nerd glasses firmly perched on her nose. They'd hooked up twice already this week and he was trying not to push for more—that body! That face!—but, hell, it was the end of the working week.

Except for Ally... *Frig*, she was still in work mode and, judging by her tight mouth, she was not amused that he'd interrupted her at six-thirty on a Friday afternoon and told her to haul her ass up to his house.

Seeing him, Ally put her hands on her hips and glared at him. 'I do not appreciate you summoning me here, disconnecting, and then not answering my return calls.'

Well, if she came willingly then he wouldn't have to summon her, would he? 'If I asked you to come for a meal, like I have the last couple of times, you'd just give me a song and dance about having work to do and brush me off.'

'I *do* have work to do! You insisted that I come to Cape Town, but that doesn't mean that the rest of my work has gone away. This isn't all I have to concentrate on!'

Ross glared at her. 'BS—you're just looking for a way to avoid spending time with me. You're okay with us sleeping together, having incredible sex, but talking is another story.'

Ally didn't make a move to come to the door. 'We don't have to talk! That was the deal.' She looked confused. 'Wasn't it?'

Ross massaged his forehead with his fingers. 'God, Jones, stop being a pain in my ass and come and have some dinner.'

'I don't know, Ross…'

'It's lasagne, not a bloody marriage proposal. Wine, food, and hopefully—but I'm not holding my breath—conversation.' Ross threw up his hands at her mutinous face. 'You know what? Do what you want. I'm going inside.'

He was halfway to the kitchen when he heard footsteps on the wooden floor and he turned to see her in the doorway, the sunlight turning her hair to a deep shade of gold. When he stepped inside, he could see her troubled face, the tension in her shoulders as she crossed her arms across her chest.

'I don't talk so well.'

He made sure to keep his voice even. 'I've heard you talk—you seem to string sentences together in a coherent way.'

Ally scrunched up her face. 'You know what I mean.'

'I don't, actually.'

She looked at the floor. 'I don't open up. I want to but I can't. And if I do then we'll go from being just a hook-up to something else.'

Ross stroked his chin. 'We'd go from a hook-up to being friends, Alyssa. There is nothing wrong with us being friends.'

'I don't have many friends,' Ally said.

From what I gather you don't have any friends, and that's not healthy, Ross thought. What had happened to make her so scared of opening up? To make her feel that it was important to be so emotionally independent? 'Maybe it's time to try.'

'Maybe.'

Progress, Ross thought. 'Just do me a favour, please?'

'What?' Ally looked wary.

'Don't keep fighting every move I make, okay? If it's

the end of a workday and I invite you out, say yes now and again—please. Begging for your time sucks.'

Ally was brave enough to meet his eyes and he saw the embarrassment and apology in them. 'Sorry.'

'Okay. Want something to drink?'

Ally nodded and he walked into the kitchen to pour them each a glass from the bottle he'd opened earlier.

'I like your house,' Ally said, taking the glass he held out to her.

'Thanks,' Ross replied, sipping the Merlot. He stood for a moment and tried to see the very familiar space with new eyes. If he looked straight ahead the passage past the stairs took him to the kitchen and a small TV lounge; to the left was the main lounge, its walls lined with glass-fronted bookcases and its ceiling a soaring double volume. The wooden doors at the far side of the room framed the sea view perfectly. Outside those doors was an outside living space and a heated lap pool that he tried to make use of most days.

With three bedrooms, and a study on the second floor, it was a ridiculous amount of space for one guy but he loved the openness, the flow, and the fact that he could more than swing a cat if he wanted to.

'Where's Pic?'

'Guy took him for a run on the beach. He was going anyway so he stopped by to pick Pic up,' Ross answered.

Unable to wait any longer to touch her, he settled his hands on Ally's shoulders and pulled her to him, resting his chin on the top of her head. She was so slight, so girly, so soft and fragrant, but so damn complicated.

Ross kept himself from doing anything but rubbing her back—okay, he copped a quick feel of her ass, but that was it. If he started he wouldn't be able to stop, and hauling her off to bed, to the couch, the floor, would undo all the good work he'd done earlier.

He stepped back, took her hand and led her to the kitchen. 'Come and help me get the food on the table.'

Ally shot him a coy look. 'I'd much rather help you with what's happening in your pants.'

His hand tightened around hers as he considered her offer. 'Oh, no, you're not getting out of conversation that easily.'

At least she'd eaten some lasagne, Ross thought as Ally pushed her plate away and lifted her wine glass. And she'd promised not to give him a hard time about his invitations. That was a win...kind of.

On another point... *Frig*, she could rock a sundress, he thought. Today's outfit was a tangerine number, warm against her olive skin, with a bare back and tied at her neck. One little tug...

Ross shifted as the fabric of his solid black board shorts tightened against the festival in his pants and rolled his eyes at himself. It was embarrassing to admit that around her he had the control of a fifteen-year-old.

While he was utterly relaxed—okay, except for down below—Ally was now acting as if she had ants in her pants. They'd taken a walk on the beach before supper and when they'd come back to the house she'd made a salad, and then they'd taken the food to the dining table on the veranda and tucked in.

Now she had her heels up on the chair, her arms wrapped around her bare legs and her fingers tapping against her arms. She was jittery as hell. Ross watched her out of the corner of his eye and wondered why she had such a hard time sitting still. Relaxing.

The only time he'd seen her truly relaxed was in his bed, after he'd given her a spectacular orgasm or two...or three or four.

Not to boast or anything.

'I'll just take the plates through,' Ally muttered, starting to stand.

'Sit down,' he said mildly, and she sank back into her chair. 'We'll take them through later. Or tomorrow.'

Ally looked at him as if he'd suggested that he toss them over the balcony.

'This is supposed to be fun, Jones,' he commented idly. 'Dinner, a spectacular sunset, wine…'

'I don't know what to do,' Ally admitted.

Ross contained his sad smile. 'You're not supposed to do anything. That's the point.'

Ally gnawed her bottom lip. 'I'm not so good at that.'

Really? He would never have guessed. Ever.

'Want to know what I think?' Ross asked, refilling their glasses.

Ally winced. 'Will I like it?'

'Probably not. You, Jones, are super-stressed, and I think that you have been for so long that you now consider this state of being to be normal.'

Ally started to protest but Ross spoke over her.

'How do you sleep? And how long does it take you to get to sleep? I bet you toss and turn while your mind races.' She always left his bed and he hated it… He had this little fantasy of waking up to Ally and rolling over and sliding home.

'Maybe.'

Maybe, her stubborn ass.

'So, not sleeping… We also know that you can be irritable and impatient.' Ross grinned at the tongue she poked out at him.

'You don't enjoy food and you can't relax. Look at you—sitting there, thinking of all the things you should be doing,' he stated. 'And we haven't even touched on the fact that you frequently put your fist to your sternum, suggesting that something unpleasant is happening below.'

Ross reached out and patted her thigh.

'But apart from those you have no symptoms of stress.'

Ross placed his glass on the table and rested his wrists on his bare knees, looking at her profile.

'What's pushing your need to work like a demon, Al? You work crazy hours, and I presume you make a pile of money that you probably don't have time to spend, you have an unhealthy relationship with anti-acid medicine and no friends. This isn't normal.'

Ally sighed, pulled her thick hair up into a rough pony-tail and secured it with the band around her wrist. 'Okay, maybe I'm a little stressed.'

And really good at avoiding the hard issues too.

'Okay, maybe I am a *lot* stressed. And maybe you are right—maybe it's become the new normal for me.'

'Those demons are winning, Jones. Do you even know what they are?'

Ross saw her throat bob and caught the flash of panic in her eyes, the sheen of emotion. But then those curtains fell in her eyes and she half turned away from him, seemingly entranced by Pic, who lay at her feet.

She bent down to rub his enormous head. 'God, he's so sweet.'

Ross felt the familiar burn of irritation as she shut down and avoided the question. Instead of just letting it slide, he was annoyed enough to shuffle his chair so that he was directly in her line of sight. 'Don't do that, okay? Don't shut down. We can't communicate if you shut down. And it pisses me off.'

'I don't want to talk about this,' Ally hissed. 'It's not relaxing me.'

'Nice try, sweetheart, but that's not going to work,' Ross retorted. 'Dammit, *talk* to me.'

Ally closed her eyes. 'Please don't do this to me. Don't push. I'm having so much fun with you and I don't want to lose you…yet.'

Ross frowned. 'I'm not going anywhere.'

Ally rubbed her forehead with the tips of her fingers. 'No, but I'll push you away. It's what I do, Ross. As soon as a guy starts to push for more…emotion, not sex…I freak out and I find a way to destroy it. I don't want to do that to you.'

Ross felt unbelievably sad at her fear-saturated words. He leaned across the table and held her jaw within his big hand. 'Well, here's a suggestion, Jones.'

'What?'

'Do something different: talk to me and don't kick me into touch.'

Ally held his eyes before shaking her head. 'What's the point, Ross? I'm here for a couple more weeks and then we'll be living our lives on two different continents. And—not meaning to be rude or to insult you—if I can't emotionally connect with my own family, why would I be able to with you? I want to…I do…but I can't.'

Ross felt stupid and ridiculous as if she'd shoved a red-hot poker through his heart. Why did that one statement have the power to suck the bones out of his spine, the blood out of his system?

He sat back and rubbed the back of his neck. 'Jones, you are a friggin' basket case.'

Ally swallowed and nodded. 'I know. So can I please take the plates to the kitchen now?'

There didn't seem to be much more to say, Ally thought as she headed for her car to go back to her apartment a little while later. She'd refused dessert and coffee, and Ross had instinctively known that she wasn't up for sex fun tonight and hadn't pushed. Instead he'd hugged her and suggested that she get a good night's sleep.

She'd felt his hand on her back and felt the unfamiliar burn of tears in her eyes. This was why she wasn't worthy of a relationship, she thought. She always managed to muck it up. It was better not to start anything because she knew that once Ross started really getting to know her— hell, once *anyone* started really getting to know her—then he would eventually reject her. She'd learnt that at her father's knee. And if *he* hadn't been able to love her, was she worthy of being loved?

Because—and nobody knew this—deep down somewhere inside she was an emotional person. Hadn't her father told her that all the time?

'You're too emotional—get a grip!'

'Waterworks again? God help me.'

'Can you at least try to cultivate some logic and reason? Think with your head and not your heart!'

Life with her father had been an emotion-free zone. She hadn't been allowed to express anger, sadness, fear. By the time she was fifteen she had come to believe that her feelings were wrong—so much so that she'd even battled to allow herself to grieve for her father, to feel scared at a lifetime to be faced without him.

She'd become stoic. And when she'd been yanked into the Bellechier household she'd kept up the habit of repressing her feelings. She didn't want to cause the Bellechiers the same trouble she'd caused her father by being emotionally unstable because, unlike her father, they didn't *have* to keep her.

And there was an even better reason for keeping her distance: if she didn't get emotionally involved she couldn't get hurt. *Yep, that works for me,* she thought as she got into her car and started it up.

In many ways she was still fifteen, still scared, still feeling unlovable, still expecting rejection. But there was a piece of her that wanted to let Ross in, that wanted to share her inner thoughts and fears with him.

She sent him an apologetic smile before lifting her hand and accelerating down the driveway.

But that was such an impossible, impossible dream because it would mean destroying that Kevlar bubble she had constructed around her heart.

To: rossbennett@rbmedia.com
From: AJones@bellechier.com
Subject: Arrangements for Thursday's shoot
Hi Ross
With regard to Thursday's shoot...

In his office at RBM Ross skimmed through Ally's e-mail, quickly realised that it was a rehash of everything she'd told him at least six times before and that it contained nothing personal—*you are a sex god* would have been nice—and deleted the message.

What was it with these corporate types that they had to check and double-check every last detail? It was as if the rest of the world couldn't function without their continuous input. It drove him nuts…

Ross lifted his head as a sharp rap sounded on his door and gestured for his CFO to enter. Gavin out-nerded even his nerdiest computer geeks, but behind the Coke-bottle-thick glasses and crappy clothes was a first-class brain.

Ross rather liked first-class brains—especially when they were working for him. 'You're looking serious,' he said, gesturing Gavin to a chair on the other side of his messy desk. 'What's up?'

'As you are well aware, due to the success of Win! you've had quite a few offers to buy out RBM.'

Ross shrugged; as with the branding issue, people wanted a piece of the hot action. 'Yeah? So? I don't want to sell.'

'Most people back off when they hear that…except for a company called Benrope. They won't hear any of the "not interested" messages I've sent and have continued to send offers to purchase. That piqued my curiosity and I did some digging.'

Ross raised his eyebrows and Gavin continued. 'Benrope is a subsidiary of Bennett Inc. Your dad wants to buy your company. I thought you should know.'

Ross closed his eyes, counted to ten, and then to twenty. When he opened them again he saw Gavin shutting his office door behind him. Benrope: Bennett, Ross, Hope. Grateful to be alone, he dialled a number he knew by heart, and realised that his father was expecting his call when he was put through almost immediately.

'Why do you want my company, Jonas?'

'I need you back here, and if buying out your company is the way to do it then that's what I'll do,' Jonas replied, his voice gravelly from a lifetime of smoking. 'I need to pass the baton.'

'I'd rather swallow cut glass.' Ross gripped the bridge of his nose with his free fingers, pushed back his chair and stared at the floor beneath his feet. No *I'm sorry*. No *Come back into the family*. Just business. All business. Always business.

Frick.

'What will it take to make you change your mind?'

Jonas used the same line Ally had, and Ross wondered if he'd missed Learn to Speak Corporate at uni or whether it was an advanced class you only got to attend when you became a bona-fide workaholic. He felt his temper bubble and pop and fought the urge to throw his phone across the room.

'I don't want anything from you. I don't need anything from you.'

'You belong here—with me,' Jonas insisted.

Like hell. 'The days when I take orders from you, or anybody, are long over.'

'You're a Bennett. I built this for you.'

'And you're still lying to yourself. You built it for yourself—to satisfy your need to be the king of the hill. Everything else was sacrificed for Bennett Inc. Mum, Hope, me.' Ross swallowed down his bile. 'When are you going to understand that I don't want your life?'

Jonas was silent for a long time. A minute? Two?

Ross was about to hang up when he spoke again, his voice low, old and frustrated. 'This is all I have to give you. I don't know what else you want.'

This was the frankest, most open conversation they'd ever had and Ross took the opportunity to say the things he'd left too long unsaid.

'I think it's too late for what I want. I wanted your time, your attention, to feel that I was more important than a business. I wanted a dad I could watch sports with, have a beer with, shoot the breeze with. Except I got you: inattentive and uninterested unless I was as involved with and as consumed by Bennett Inc. as you. It was too high a price to pay. It will always be too high a price.'

'I don't know what to say to that.'

'There is nothing to say, Jonas. Tell your minions at Benrope to stop annoying my CFO with buy-out offers. It's never going to happen.'

Ross very gently and very deliberately placed the receiver into its cradle—he was *not* going to allow his father to make him lose his temper!—and jumped to his feet. Moving over to his window, he opened it wide, allowing the air-conditioned air to rush out while he sucked in fresh, clean air.

Jonas... Talking with him was always such a pleasure.

Ross heard his phone beep the arrival of a text message and pulled it out of his pocket. Ally.

It's nearly three o'clock. Time to leave. Don't be late. We're on a tight schedule.

Irritation welled again, hard and true. Another work-obsessed, stubborn-ass, anal corporate drone. Sexy as hell, though. Unfortunately.

CHAPTER TEN

ROSS PARKED HIS Ducati next to the stairs leading up to Ally's apartment and yanked off his helmet. What a God-awful crappy day, he thought, and he still had to walk a little way up Table Mountain with a fake girlfriend and play nice with the cameras.

Kill me now, he thought, kicking down the stand and climbing off the bike. It was ridiculous how one conversation with his father could derail his mood, make him feel off balance and pull all those stupid feelings of disappointment and resentment to the surface.

His father was an emotional moron, he thought in disgust as he headed for the stairs. So why did he still wish he could have a proper relationship with the man? Why did he still seek his approval? Maybe *he* was the moron, he thought as he climbed the stairs, wishing he'd taken a handful of aspirin before he left the office. His head felt as if it was ready to explode...

Thanks, Dad.

Ross felt his mobile vibrate in his pocket and pulled it out to squint at the screen. Ally...of course it was.

WTH are you????

Frick. Why did he have to deal with two managing, corporate, controlling personalities in one day?

Deciding to jerk her chain, he quickly formulated a reply.

Why? Did we have plans?

Because, really, he needed sixty reminders to get something in his head.

Don't mess with me, Bennett! I'm not in the mood.

Ross jerked that chain again.

Let's compare days, sweetheart. Bet I'll win. I'll be there in an hour. Some bugs in a string code that we need to sort out.

Ross stood outside her door and waited, knowing that it was coming. Five, four, three…and his mobile rang in his hand. That was the problem with control freaks and people with tunnel vision—it made their actions easy to predict. It was a lesson he'd learnt the hard way with Jonas. Along with 'Do it my way or get the hell out of my life'.

He'd chosen to get the hell out…but, man, he still wished that there had been a middle ground.

Ross shook his head and walked into the apartment, waving his ringing mobile and rolling his eyes.

'You really should trust people more, Jones,' he said.

She didn't look happy with him and Ross silently suggested that she get in line.

Ally watched Ross's long-length stride as he made his way past the clothing racks and camera equipment to her side, his hair pulled back from his face. His eyes were hard, his mouth unyielding, and tension had his shoulders up around his ears. Okay, so he wasn't having a good day. Well, she wasn't having a good *week*.

Ross's mobile chirped and while she waited for him to finish his call she mused over the fact that her time in Cape Town work-wise had been eye-opening. Trying to plan and organise a shoot in a strange city was always a challenge, and Cape Town was no different.

Half of the Bellechier collection of clothing and accessories for Ross was still in Customs and Ally was struggling to get it released. Their cameraman had flu, and for some reason her normally crazily efficient, focused and dedicated crew—from both Bellechier *and* the ad agency—were treating this shoot as a working holiday.

They dressed for work as if they were heading for the beach, sloped off early to watch the whales or to visit one of the nearby wine farms. Didn't they realise how important this campaign was? How essential it was that everything had to be perfect?

The chances of this going badly wrong were stratospheric—Ross was a gamble, teaming his bad-ass CEO look with the upmarket but casual clothes of the new line was a gamble, and shooting the commercials in Cape Town was a gamble—and she didn't like to gamble when it came to Bellechier or her job.

She liked certainties, plans, a clear route to the goal… and she definitely didn't like the fact that she was frequently distracted from said goal by thoughts of Ross…in and out of the bedroom.

Ross disconnected and jammed his mobile back into his pocket. Such a heart-grabbingly handsome man, she thought, with his wizard eyes, grim mouth and short hair… Dear Lord, he'd cut his shoulder-length hair.

What. The. Hell?

Noooooooo…

'You've cut your hair,' Ally whimpered, her hand swiping her mouth in horror.

Ross ran a hand over his short, spiky head. 'Yeah, I thought I should tidy it up before the filming started.'

'And you didn't think to talk to me about it?' Ally demanded, completely and utterly horrified.

'I've been making decisions about my hair for a while now—without your input,' Ross replied, his voice hard.

She was too appalled to hear the warning note in it.

Dammit, sod it… He'd cut his hair. There went the jux-taposition between her bad-boy CEO and the sophisticated Bellechier clothes. How would it affect the campaign? Would it hurt it? Would it fail? Would she fail? *Dammit, Bennett!*

'Yeah but since you sold your face, your hair, to Bellech-ier—to me!—then I should've been consulted!' Ally twisted her hands together. 'What were you *thinking*?'

Unaware that the six other people in the room were watching their argument with interest and amusement, Ally jumped when Ross grabbed her arm and hauled her across to the door that led to a deck outside. He pushed her through the open door, slammed it shut behind her and walked her down the deck so that they were out of earshot of the rest of the crew.

Ally wrenched her arm from his grasp. 'What are you doing? I'm not some cave girl you can drag around!'

'And I'm not someone you get to shout at. And let me tell you something else, Jones: I never sold a damn thing to you *or* Bellechier! So don't you ever speak to me like that again!' he said in a low, frustrated voice.

Ally felt the burn in her gut, the all too familiar pain beneath her ribs. 'Well, you shouldn't have cut your hair!'

'It's *my* bloody hair!'

Ross linked his hands behind his head and sucked in a deep breath, obviously looking for control. His eyes sparked dangerously.

'You need to start treating me like an intelligent human being—and that includes you not sending me a dozen e-mails about the same blasted thing!—or we call it quits right now. I *do* run a multi-frickin'-mega-million-dollar company, you know, and I do not need your constant memos and re-minders! It's about time you and everyone else realised that I'm pretty damn good at organising my life!'

Jeez! Where had that come from?

'I'm just trying to make sure everything runs smoothly,' Ally protested, her temper fizzing. 'This is my job, Ross!'

'Well, this is my life, so butt the hell out!'

Okay, this was the first time she'd seen him angry—really angry. Suddenly Ally wasn't even sure what they were arguing about.

'You're micro-managing me and you're driving me nuts. Your staff must be on Prozac, dealing with you every day. You'd drive a monk to meth, Alyssa!'

That was harsh and cruel. And very unlike the Ross she'd thought she—kind of—knew.

Norm, the creative director for the ad agency, stuck his head around the corner of the deck and shuffled his feet. 'Sorry to interrupt your screaming match, but if we don't leave within the next five minutes we're going to run out of light…and time.'

Ross nodded tersely. He gestured to Ally and in a hard, cold voice asked, 'Do you need *her* there?'

Norm looked uncomfortable and Ally sighed.

'Why?' he asked.

'Because I want to get this done, and it would go a hell of a lot quicker and easier if she wasn't bitching at me.'

'That's so unfair,' Ally said in a low voice, hurt twisting her stomach and piercing her heart.

Ross ignored her. 'Well?' he demanded, still looking at Norm.

'We could do it without her,' Norm said, with an apologetic look in her direction. He held up his hand in protest. 'This time.'

'Stay here,' Ross commanded her.

Ally really, *really* didn't respond well to orders. She slapped her hands on her hips and lifted her chin. 'And if I don't?'

'Alyssa, just give me a goddamn break…please?' He looked at Norm. 'What's your name?'

'Norm. Creative Director.'

'Ok…Norm and I are going to get this done and we'll talk later. Maybe.'

Ross brushed past Ally and stormed back into the room,

and Ally surmised that he must have issued a quick command because everyone in the room started moving, gathering clothes and equipment as they went.

Norm cleared his throat and Ally turned to look at him, her lips pursed.

'Sorry, Ally.'

'Not your fault, hon.' Ally shoved her hands into her hair. 'I guess I lit the fuse to that particular powder keg.'

Norm placed his hands on her shoulders. 'We'll get it done, Al.'

Ally nodded and dredged up a smile. 'You always do. Thanks, Norm.'

Ross poked his head around the door, glared at them both and snapped out his parting shot. 'I'm leaving. You coming or staying, Norm?'

Hours later Ally stood on the wooden deck of the apartment, her arms on the railing, a half-empty wine glass dangling from her fingers, and stared out at the restless Atlantic ocean. Ross's words bounced around her head. Was she *really* such a micro-manager? *Did* her staff need Prozac? *Would* she drive a monk to meth?

Was she really that bad? In her quest for perfection, her desire to succeed, did she treat people like fools? Lord, she hoped not. But she suspected—knew—that she did sometimes. She could be hell on her staff—was definitely hell on relationships. But Ross was the first person to call her on it…the first man to point out her faults and to tell her that her behaviour was unacceptable.

She didn't like it but she had to respect it. Ally frowned into the darkness. She really didn't like the fact that he'd kept her off the shoot. She wouldn't allow that to happen again.

'Thinking of ways to off me?'

Ally jumped and whirled round, her heart threatening to climb out of her chest and belt off into the darkness. Ross stood on the other side of the deck, his shoulder on the glass and wood door that led back into the apartment.

'How did you get in?' she asked, placing her wine glass on the low coffee table beneath her.

'Norm gave me his key. He said to tell you that I was on my best behaviour and that the shoot went well.' Ross held up his hand as she looked around for her mobile. 'He also said to tell you that he's switching his phone off and that he'll fill you in tomorrow.' Ross pulled the pad of his thumb along his chin. 'So, about this afternoon…'

Ally stared out to sea, every muscle in her body taut with tension. 'I'm sorry I shouted at you. I'm especially sorry that I did it front of the entire crew.'

Ross was quiet for so long that Ally eventually made herself look at him. Even in the low light she could see the upward tilt of his lips.

'Bet that hurt,' he said finally.

She knew that she had more to say and fumbled for the words. 'I was wrong, but you shouldn't have banned me from the shoot.'

Ross nodded and Ally was surprised.

'You're right, that was a low blow. As were the Prozac and meth-addicted monk comments.' Ross rubbed the back of his neck as he walked across the deck in her direction. He gripped the railing with his hands and dropped his head back to look at the stars.

'What do you know about my dad?'

The question came out of the blue and Ally had to take a moment to catch up. 'Uh…thinking… Not much, actually. He's never spoken publicly about how and why he built Bennett Inc., has he?'

'That's my dad; for an owner of a PR company he's not great at communicating.' Ross took a sip of wine from her glass on the table and gestured for her to sit down on the square ottoman that ran the length of the deck. Ally dropped down, crossed her legs and rested her elbows on her knees.

Ross sat down next to her, leaned his back against the railing and casually draped his forearm across her knee.

'He grew up poor—very poor—and he vowed that his children would want for nothing. Ever.' Ross's voice was as deep and dark as the night. 'We didn't. My sister and I had the latest toys, the latest clothes, the best education. What we didn't have was his time, his attention, his input. We never felt loved, and we always felt like we were competing with Bennett Inc. We always lost.'

Ally knew that platitudes and sympathy would be unwelcome so she gave him silence and waited until he spoke again.

'I thought that by going to work with him at Bennett Inc., by sharing his work, we would have something we could build a relationship on. I never banked on how much I would hate it.'

'Why did you hate it so much?'

Ross let out a long breath. 'It's soulless. So many rules, written and unwritten, and none of them serve any purpose. The corporate world is about the bottom line, and people are a casualty of getting those profits. It was sucking the life out of me—and, trust me, I had it easy. My father made sure of that. When I felt like I couldn't breathe any more I bailed and my father didn't take it well.'

'What happened?'

'He cut me off. From everything.' Ross's hand gripped her knee. 'A lot of people within the company and probably within our extended family think that our rift is about the fact that he cut me off from my trust fund, from the family money... Hell, I wouldn't be surprised if Jonas still thought that too.'

'It wasn't about the money because *you're* not about the money,' Ally murmured.

A look of quick appreciation flashed across his face. 'I'm really not. Money is a tool, not a goal. I didn't want to work in a corporate environment. I wanted to do something creative—be someone other than Jonas Bennett's son. Jonas couldn't understand that—that Bennett Inc. was his baby, not mine.'

Ross finished her wine and Ally let him. He needed it a lot more than she did at the moment.

'This afternoon I found out that he's been trying to buy RBM to leverage me into coming back to run Bennett Inc. We had an argument which set my teeth on edge. And then I came here and you…'

'Laid into you about your hair.' Ally shook her head. 'I might have said it badly but I'm still pretty unhappy that you cut it, Bennett.'

'Because you had a look in mind for the ads?'

Ally put her hand on his jaw and pushed his cheek so that he was facing her. 'No, because long hair suited you. Because that was the way you chose to wear it. Because you liked it. I never wanted to make you into something you aren't, Ross. You're a long haired, stubble-toting bad-ass CEO and that's who I wanted to show the world. But dressed up in pretty clothes.'

Ross stared at her for a long minute.

Ally dropped her hand and smiled. 'No worries. The face is still good. I texted the stylist to make sure that it was as messy as possible on the shoot. But keep the stubble, okay?'

Ross rubbed his jaw. 'No worries about that. I've never had a problem growing a beard.'

Ally moved so that she sat next to him, her shoulder against his upper arm. Ross put his arm around her and pulled her in close. 'Ross…'

'Mmm?'

'Maybe later, when you're feeling calmer, you might look beyond your father's words and try and see what he could be saying by his attempts to get you back to Bennett Inc. Maybe entrusting you with the thing he loves most—his company—is his way of telling you that he loves you, of making amends. Maybe he just doesn't know how else to say it…'

'But I don't want it.'

'And maybe he would accept that if you acknowledged his gift, his trust in you, before you said no. Maybe that's all you need to do.'

Ross didn't say anything and Ally eventually felt his kiss on her temple.

'Maybe.'

Ally smiled as his big hand held her head against his chest and they listened to the waves crashing on the beach.

They were doing a photo shoot in Ross's office, and perfectionist Ally winced at the messy desk, the basketball hoop on the wall and the battered leather couch that Ross was currently lying on, laptop on his knees, totally at ease as the photographer moved in front of him and the camera whirled.

'Cross your legs at the ankles,' Bert told him, dropping to one knee and twisting his body to get the shot he needed.

Ross, dressed in charcoal and white striped pants and a matching waistcoat, which the stylist had placed over a snow-white T-shirt that hugged his shoulders and bicep, looked delicious.

Ally really, *really* wished he hadn't cut his hair.

Everyone in the room except the photographer turned at a knock on the door.

'I don't want to be disturbed!' Bert shouted.

'Dude—my office, my rules,' Ross said in a calm voice that did not encourage argument. He looked over his shoulder as Eli pushed his way past Ally to look down at Ross.

Ally noticed that Eli didn't seem remotely concerned or surprised that Ross was doing a shoot.

'We've hit a major snag with the Japanese build.' He bounced on his feet, worry rolling off him in waves. 'The interface isn't talking to the hardware.'

Ross twisted his lips. 'Okay.'

'It's not okay! They are flying in tomorrow afternoon for the demo and we have nothing to demo!'

Ross swung his feet off the couch and sat up. He gave Eli a small smile. 'How long have you and your team been up?'

Eli tapped his fingers against his thigh. 'We didn't sleep last night.'

'Yeah—there's your problem. Tell the boys to go home, get something to eat—'

'But the build…'

''E, you're exhausted. You couldn't work out square roots at the moment. Come back fresh early tomorrow morning and start again.' Ross lifted a powerful shoulder. 'I guarantee that you'll find the solution in ten minutes in the morning.'

'Jeez, Ross…I don't know. Don't you want to come and talk it through with us?'

'No, I pay you and your team a wicked salary to get it right; that's your job, not mine. Go home. I don't want to see any of you here until you've had a solid eight.' Ross lifted his eyebrows and held Eli's eyes.

Ally saw Eli's nod and caught the quick look of relief on Ross's face. He cared about his staff and he managed them well.

'What happens if they don't solve the problem?' Ally asked him when Eli had left the room.

Ross looked up at her. 'They will. They are the best there is; they're just tired and stressed—and who can be effective when they are living like that?'

Ally knew that his raised eyebrows were for her and she wiggled under his direct look. She liked the way he managed his people—giving them space to do their jobs, support when they needed it—and, as she'd witnessed earlier, when she'd walked in on Ross giving his interns a rollicking, he knew how to wield the big stick as well.

He actually *managed* his people while she, she suspected, either hovered until the task was perfected or simply removed the project and did it herself.

Not healthy, she thought, or clever.

Ross, ignoring the photographer's yelp of protest, stood up and moved towards her to hold her face in his hands. He bent his knees so that his eyes were level with hers.

'You've got to learn to trust your people, Jones,' he said, before dropping a quick kiss on her mouth.

'Can we get back to work now?' Bert complained.

Kate, the pink-haired girl, popped her head into his office. 'Ross, I need a minute.'

Ross grinned as Bert groaned and waved her in. He took the next set of clothes that the stylist held out to him and jerked his head towards the bathroom. 'I'll leave the door open a crack so that you can talk.'

Kate sent Ally a naughty grin. 'Damn, I was hoping to catch a glimpse of you naked.'

Ally gave Ross a heated look before laughing. 'Trust me, it's as good as you imagine.'

Ally and Ross sat on the beach below his house, a bottle of red pushed into the soft sand, their backs against a large piece of driftwood. It was that magical hour between afternoon and nightfall...

'I don't like the word *dusk*—it doesn't capture the essence, the magic of this time of day,' Ally stated quietly. 'The air is so still and fragrant, the waves are almost lazy, the sun is sinking slowly...'

Ross leaned forward and twisted his torso to send her a quizzical look. 'Right...who are you and what have you done with logical and practical Ally?'

Ally swatted his shoulder with the back of her hand. 'Funny man. I wasn't always buttoned down and repressed, you know.'

'I know that... Anyone who is as passionate as you in the sack is at heart warm and emotional.'

Somehow Ross had managed to see past workaholic Ally to the person she'd used to be. Ally wasn't sure whether that scared the crap out of her or made her feel warm and fuzzy.

Both, probably.

'I have reasons for being practical and logical, Ross,' she stated quietly.

'Ready to tell me what they are?'

Was she? She didn't know if 'ready' was the right word. She didn't know if she'd ever be ready to expose herself like that. It was as scary as hell, but she wanted to crack the door open, to let him in...

Maybe just to prove to herself that she could.

'My father was a stoic, practical, unemotional man who didn't know how to raise or relate to a little girl. He loved me—I know he did—he just didn't *get* me. I was an emotional child—either wildly happy or crazy sad. I'd weep for days if I found a dead bird or laugh like crazy at a book or a comic or a TV show.' Ally rolled the stem of her wine glass between her hands. 'He couldn't deal with either. He wanted...*needed* peace. He had a hugely stressful job and couldn't cope with much more at the end of the day— couldn't cope with me.'

Ally heard Ross swear, knew he was thinking badly of her father and needed to protect him.

'As I said—he loved me, Ross. He just didn't know how to handle me. As I grew up I realised that every time I showed emotion he retreated, but when I managed to control those emotions he could engage with me. I wanted his attention so I controlled my emotions. By the time I was thirteen I'd learnt to look outside of what I was feeling to the logic and practicality of the situation.' Ally smiled quickly. 'I was one hell of a debater.'

'I just bet you were,' Ross muttered, refilling their wine glasses.

'He died on a beach in Phuket. I was with him,' Ally said in a low, calm voice. 'Justin and Sabine had bullied him into taking a holiday—sound familiar?—and I came out of the water and he was dead.' Her breathing became shallow and spots danced behind her eyes.

'I've got you,' Ross said in his deep, stable voice.

Ally felt his arm around her, anchoring her, and pulled in a couple of deep breaths. 'I've never told anyone this, so just hang on while I blurt it all out. There was a lot of confusion. I think I screamed and people ran to us. Somebody tried to give him CPR but I kept getting in their way, yelling at him to wake up. The police came. I remember lots of people in uniform. There was the language problem—it was Thailand—and I remember going to a police station and nobody quite knowing what to do with me for the longest time.'

Ross urged her to sip her wine, which she did, and she felt the tart liquid slide down her dry throat.

'Eventually they allowed me to go back to my hotel room with a young Thai policewoman to look after me. She didn't speak any English so she watched Thai TV and ordered Room Service. Someone came from the British Embassy and asked me a million questions, some of which I managed to answer. I was told to hang on, that they were working on what to do with me.'

Ally shuddered.

'I was so scared, Ross. I was in a foreign country in a hotel room and I'd just lost my dad. I thought that I'd end up in some Thai orphanage. After two or three days the fear just got to me and I think I shut down. When the man from the embassy came back I couldn't talk to him—couldn't speak at all. My vocal cords were literally frozen in fear. I was too scared to eat, drink, bathe.'

Ally yelped as Ross grabbed her and yanked her onto his lap, holding her against him and burying his face in her hair. She patted his arm in an attempt to reassure him. Or was it herself? Did it matter?

'I'm not sure how long it took—it felt like years—but then Justin and Sabine came and I could breathe again. I knew that I was safe.'

Pic crawled up to them and laid his head on Ally's thigh, whining at her distress. Ally immediately reached out to rub his head.

After a long time, Ross spoke again. 'But you've never allowed yourself to really be part of their family. They love you, Al, so why not?'

Ally heard the reassuring thump of his heart and sifted

through the words, picking up and discarding phrases until she found the right ones. 'When the man from the embassy came to tell me that Justin and Sabine were on their way he suggested that I not give them any trouble. I shouldn't make waves. He said that they could return me to the system at any point.'

Ross growled. 'Bastard.'

Ally shrugged. 'He just reinforced what I'd already been taught. I didn't want to risk losing them. I'd already lost my mother and father and I didn't think I could—don't think I can—lose someone else I love. Anyway, I'd already learnt to shut down my emotions with my dad so I thought that was what they expected too. It was safer to be disconnected, Ross—it still is.'

'But it's not healthy.'

'That's a matter of perspective,' Ally replied. 'You've called me a basket case before, Ross, but you just never quite realised quite how well I fit the bill.'

Ross's arms tightened around her but he ignored her comment. 'So why do you work so hard?'

'Partly to repay the Bellechiers for taking me into their home. Partly because it keeps me from thinking. Mostly because it's the one place where the world approves of logic and practicality, where emotion has no place.' Ally tipped her head back to look up into his gorgeous face. 'I've never told anyone else this, Ross.'

'Why did you tell me?'

Ally shrugged. 'I'm not actually sure.'

'Oh, Alyssa.' Ross rubbed his chin in her hair. 'I think the truth is that you want to reconnect with your emotions, with yourself, and this might be the first step. But you should be doing this with your family, Al, with Sabine.'

And not with me... Ally heard the unspoken words and she knew that they were truth personified. He was temporary—a lovely, lovely diversion—but he wasn't long term. She would be going back to Geneva and he would be

staying in Cape Town and in time he would be a wonderful memory.

She didn't want him to be a memory but how could he be
anything else? She was so not his type. And there was the
little hurdle of there being all of Africa and a fair chunk of
Europe between them.

'I think you deserve more from life than the half-life
you are living. I think you are too smart, have too much to
give, to waste your life at work. You have too much passion inside to spend it alone.' Ross rubbed his hand across
her back. 'Start with Sabine, Al, be brave and let her in.'

CHAPTER ELEVEN

THE FOLLOWING MORNING Ally was sitting on Ross's veranda, working on her laptop, while Ross surfed on the beach below the house. She wasn't making a lot of progress because she kept thinking of their conversation the night before and how Ross had made sweet, tender, passionate love to her afterwards.

She didn't have much time left in this country; the shooting for the commercials was finished and the studio shots were scheduled for tomorrow and the next day. She was due to fly back to Geneva on Thursday and then this…this thing with Ross would come to a slamming stop. Just the thought of leaving made her want to dry heave.

When had he become so important? When had she lost her grip on her emotions and her distance? The first time she'd met him? The second? From the moment they met he'd challenged all her preconceptions about her career, her life. He made her think and, worse, he made her dream.

Was he right? she asked herself, lifting her cup of coffee to her lips. Was she wasting herself, wasting her life, spending all her time at work, keeping herself closed off and living scared?

She wanted to live a more balanced life, she admitted. Dammit, she wanted to have a life. But she didn't want a life that didn't have Ross in it. She couldn't imagine a life that didn't have Ross in it.

She wasn't sure what love felt like, what love was, but

she'd never felt like this before. Safe and thrilled in equal measure, challenged and accepted at the same time. Ally pushed her hair back from her face and, as always, logic floated to the surface.

Was she just feeling…*attached* to Ross because he was the first to give her a taste of what she was missing from her life: fun, a man, passion…fun? Was she projecting her feelings on him because he'd breached her defences? Was she feeling affection because the thought of throwing herself back into dating made her want to break out in hives?

Ally dug deep, thought of going back to Geneva, and her heart belted away into the deepest, darkest corner of her ribcage. She couldn't imagine not talking to him, not making love to him, not having him in her life.

Maybe this psychotic, thrilling, heart-thumping feeling in her stomach and heart and throat was love. It sure as hell was something…

Ally heard the doorbell ring and frowned. Standing up, she peered over the railing and looked out to sea. Immediately she saw Ross sitting on his board, waiting for a wave. Okay, so she'd answer his door.

Ally walked back through his lounge, moved a pair of his trainers out of her path—the man left shoes and clothes everywhere—and touched the wooden statue of a monstrous head at the door before yanking the door open.

Ross's face in thirty years stared back at her. 'I'm looking for Ross Bennett. I was given this address.'

Ally held out her hand. 'I'm Ally, Ross's…'

Ross's what? Girlfriend? Lover? Temporary fling? Colleague?

'Ross's friend. Come on in. He's out surfing but he should be up soon. Would you like some coffee?'

On the deck, Ross rinsed his board, pulled off his vest and draped it over the railing, then wrapped a towel around his wet board shorts. After rinsing off his feet he slid open the door and walked into the house, looking for sex and food. Or food and sex.

Either would work.

'Jones? Get off your computer, sweetheart, and let's make breakfast and fool around.'

Ross stepped through the doorway to his kitchen and raised his eyebrows as he saw someone sitting at the breakfast bar, Ally on the other side of him. He sighed... company... Dear God in heaven—the company was his father.

What the hell...? Ross sent Ally an accusing look.

She lifted her eyebrows and her hands. 'What? He rang the bell!'

Ross folded his arms across his chest and asked the only question he could. 'Jonas, what are you doing here?'

'I was hoping to talk to you...face to face.'

'Why? What can you say to me that we didn't cover on the phone the other day?' Ross demanded, feeling the old feelings of disappointment and resentment bubble up. 'You want me to come back to Bennett Inc. I would rather chew my wrists off. You wasted a trip.' He sent Ally a cold look. 'You saw him in—you can see him out. When I get out of the shower, I want him gone.'

Ross turned around and ran up the stairs to his bedroom and headed straight for the shower. All he'd wanted, he thought as hot water pounded his head, was sex and food.

Trust his father to kill his appetite for both.

When he walked out of the bathroom, a towel around his hips, Ally was sitting on the edge of his perfectly made bed—of course she couldn't leave it in a tangled mess— looking stubborn. *Here comes the lecture*, he thought.

'I don't want to hear it,' he told her, heading for his dressing room and grabbing a pair of jeans and a T-shirt.

'Tough,' Ally said as she crossed her legs. 'He flew out here to talk to you. That took courage and determination and the least you can do is hear him out.'

'It'll be the same old story.'

'Maybe, but you can't assume that.'

Ross pulled on his underwear and jeans, quickly buttoning the fly. After pulling on the T-shirt, he ran his hands through his short hair.

'Why the hell did I cut my hair? He *hated* my long hair!'

Ally grinned. 'You sound like your sixteen-year-old self. Trust me—knowing you, I'm pretty sure you'll find something to say to annoy him.' Her smile died and her eyes darkened with pain. 'A day doesn't go by when I don't wish I could see my dad again, Ross, as difficult and reserved as he was. Go and talk to him. Please?'

He twisted his lips. 'Dammit, but you are pain in my ass.'

Ally stood up and kissed his cheek. 'So you keep telling me. I'll hang on up here for a while to give you some privacy.'

Ross couldn't stop staring at Jonas. 'What the hell do you mean, you're selling Bennett Inc.?'

They'd moved to the veranda, where Ross felt he could breathe.

Jonas sat in one of the plump couches, his coffee on the table in front of him, his eyes on the view. 'Hell of a place you have here, son.'

He couldn't remember when his father had last called him son. Ross, normally the brightest lightbulb in the room, was struggling to keep up. 'Whoa, back up! You're selling the company?'

'Yep.'

'Why, for God's sake? You *love* Bennett Inc.'

Jonas slanted him a look that he couldn't interpret. 'Well, you don't want it, and Hope isn't interested either. What's the point of carrying on with it? I only built it for the two of you, and neither of you want it, so it can be sold.'

'But…but what are you going to do?'

He couldn't imagine his father not working. It was like trying to imagine a rap star without bling.

'Your mother and I are buying a boat and we're going sailing. Do you know she already got her skipper's licence?'

What? The? Fudge?

'Uh…no…'

Jonas stretched his arms out along the back of the couch and grinned. 'Last week—the day before we spoke—she told me that, with or without me, she was going sailing. I could either go along or stay. I'm choosing to go.'

Ross just stared at him, mute with shock.

'I'll give you the account number and the access codes for the bank account I've set up. Then you can bail your mother out when she ends up in a foreign jail for chopping me up with an axe,' Jonas joked.

Ross just stared at him. Who was this man who was cracking jokes and looking relaxed? It sure wasn't the up-tight father he remembered.

'Your mother made me choose. The company or her.'

Go, Mum, Ross thought, as proud as hell of his tiny mother.

'After our last discussion I realised that I'd sacrificed everything important to me—you and your sister, possibly your mother—for a business nobody cares about. It was suddenly too big a price to pay.'

Holy crap, Ross thought.

'Close your mouth,' Jonas suggested. 'There are flies about. And talking about money…'

'I don't want a damn cent,' Ross said, pushing the words out between his teeth as Jonas pushed his favourite button.

'Tough!' Jonas said on a sharkish grin. 'I've reinstated your trust fund and when the sale goes through it's going to be seriously fat. Use it…don't use it…give it away. I don't care.'

Jonas leaned forward and his face was suddenly serious and…*sincere*. Ross almost didn't recognise the expression— had he ever seen sincerity on his father's face before?

'All I care about is whether you'll accept my apology for being a…how did your mother put it?…a total dipstick.'

'Uh…'

Jonas rubbed his hand over his grey hair. 'I was hoping to avoid this part. Okay, if I have to say it, then… Hell.'

He pulled out a piece of paper from his shirt pocket. 'Your mother made me write it down.' He opened up the paper and extended his arm to squint at the words. 'I'm sorry for being a crap father, for not allowing you to follow your own path, for—'

Ross laughed, snatched the paper from his hand, crumpled it and tossed it over his shoulder. 'I think that's more than enough of Mum's soppiness.'

'Thank God. But I am very proud of what you've achieved… on your own.'

Jonas smiled and Ross ignored the sheen of emotion in their eyes.

'Well, so…I really like this house. I can see myself spending some time here. I also like the idea of Crazy Collaborations. Need some help with that?'

Ross thought for a moment. He didn't have enough time to spend on his think tank project and it could only benefit from his father's excellent business brain. It would also give Jonas something to do instead of driving his mum nuts on the boat.

'I'd be grateful for your long distance away, e-mail-based help on one condition.'

'What's that?'

'You keep your nose out of RBM.'

'Deal,' Jonas quickly agreed.

Ross, his brain working overtime at the thought of having his father back in his life, guilt-free, sat down on the chair opposite Jonas and placed his bare feet on the table. He smiled when Jonas slipped off his shoes and copied his actions.

'So, tell me about Ally. How long have you been together?' Jonas asked.

Ross slanted him a look. While he was thrilled that he and his father seemed to have turned a very steep corner, he wasn't anywhere near able to discuss his love life with him.

'Don't get excited, Jonas. She's temporary—a fling.

We're just having a bit of fun until she goes home. She's
not important.'

Ross felt his stomach clench at the lie and realised that
speaking the words didn't make them true. Ally was getting to be just the opposite; she'd slipped under his skin
and he had no idea how he was going to find the strength
to wave her goodbye.

There was nothing they could do, he thought, and it was
never going to work out. Her career, her life was in Geneva,
and he could never ask her to give it up and move to Cape
Town to be with him. After what she'd told him last night
that would be too big an ask of her.

And *he* couldn't give up RBM. He'd worked so damn
hard, and he had people relying on him—clients, customers,
staff who'd relocated, changed their lives to work for him.

Love, he realised as regret clutched his heart and
squeezed, couldn't conquer everything.

*She's temporary—a fling. We're just having a bit of fun until
she goes home. She's not important.*

She hadn't been eavesdropping—well, maybe a bit.

Ally had instinctively backed away from the door leading
to the veranda and when she was certain that Ross wouldn't
hear her footsteps had dashed up the stairs to Ross's room.

She'd had to leave—needed to be out of his house before
he saw her wet eyes and her obvious distress. Now, a couple
of hours later, back in her apartment at Camps Bay, she kept
calling herself a fool. She'd been thinking about how Ross
had changed her life, how awful it would be when she left
and how much she'd miss him—and all the time he'd considered her to be nothing more than a casual fling.

If there were awards for chronic stupidity she would be
a right up there in the running. So they'd shared a couple of
confidences? It seemed that meant nothing in the scheme of
things; Ross wasn't on the same page as her.

Hell, he wasn't even reading the same book.

Ally heard the entry buzzer, walked into the kitchen and

looked at the small screen above the intercom. There was Ross, looking dark and dangerous on his solid black Ducati. She pressed the button to allow the gate to slide open and realised that she had about a minute to get her crazy, bruised emotions under control. She couldn't allow him to know that his words to his father, so casually uttered, had made her feel as if he'd scraped out her insides with a teaspoon.

She hauled in a deep breath and pushed her hair off her face. She would be cool and in control; she would not melt into a puddle at his feet. This was the problem with feelings, she thought, they were wild and upsetting and left you feeling out of control.

Her father had been right all along: it was better to keep them all locked down. It didn't hurt that way.

'Hey,' Ross said as he walked into the airy, light-filled apartment.

Ally knew that he was walking over to kiss her so she popped around to the other side of the dining room table, which she was using as a massive desk.

'Hi,' she replied, staring down at her screen. 'Bert sent me the photographs of the office shoot…they're good. Do you want to take a look?'

Ross sent her a quizzical look. 'Uh…' He perched his butt on the corner of the table and stretched out his long legs. 'So, that was my dad.'

Dear Lord, he wanted to talk about it. She didn't think she could—not without revealing how devastated she felt. She'd started to hand over her heart, only to find out that he wasn't interested in it, and now he wanted to *talk* about it?

She didn't think so.

'We have one more photo shoot scheduled but I don't think it's necessary. I've already identified five images I want to use for the print campaign.'

'I'm thrilled,' Ross deadpanned.

Ally risked a quick look at him and sighed when she saw his narrowed eyes, his set jaw.

'What's going on, Alyssa?'

Alyssa. He only called her that when he wanted her to know that he was being deadly serious and when he wanted to get his point across. Jones was for teasing and Al was for affection. Sweetheart was for flat-out fun.

Ally licked her lips and tried to pull off an I-don't-know-what-you-mean shrug.

'Are you really going to stand there and not ask me what happened with my dad?' Ross demanded.

'Um…yeah.' Because that would be opening up a can of six-foot worms and she would lose it…

'It's what a lover would do. Or even a friend,' Ross pointed out, his hard tone layering confusion and hurt.

The fact that she had the ability to hurt him—even as a friend—made her feel off balance. And so, so sad.

But they weren't lovers—hadn't he said so? She was nothing. She wasn't important. And she'd rather poke a hot stick in her eye than let him see what that meant to her.

Ally lifted her chin high enough to make her nose bleed. 'I never signed on for the emotional stuff, Ross.'

Ross looked at her for a long time before speaking again. 'I thought we'd kicked uptight, bitchy Alyssa into touch.'

She had—or at least she'd wanted to—but she'd rather Ross think that she was cold and unfeeling than know that she was hurt and humiliated. 'Since I'm leaving in a couple days, does the way I act matter? This will be over soon anyway.'

'And if I said that I'd like to make it work?'

'I wouldn't believe you,' Ally shot back.

He was sending too many mixed messages and her head was whirling.

She shoved her hands into her hair and held her head. 'Why would you even say that, Ross? It makes absolutely no sense. Even if I believed you—which I so don't—how would we make it work? Two continents, two careers—'

'You could—'

Ally pounced on his words before he could complete that

sentence. 'Don't you *dare* ask me to sacrifice my career for yours. Do not even *go* there!'

Ross pursed his lips. 'I was going to say that you could fly here occasionally and I could go to Geneva. We have the means to do that. But I suppose that's a moot point, given that you don't seem to want to entertain the idea of an "us" beyond this fling.'

Ross placed both hands on the dining room table and looked at Ally with hard eyes.

'It's so bloody ironic that on the day that one weight is lifted off my shoulder another one falls and it's the same bloody thing. Once again I'm loving somebody who doesn't love me more than they love their job. And I'm back to feeling hurt and resentful because there's this person in my life who's emotionally unavailable, cut off, and a royal pain in my ass. I'm seriously starting to question my own sanity.'

Had he said that he loved her? Ally felt her heart jump… No, surely not. That wasn't possible…

'Everything I love is in Geneva—my family and my work. That's what's important.'

'Everything?' Ross demanded. 'Come on, Alyssa. *Everything?*'

'Where is this coming from, Ross?' Ally demanded. 'One minute we're having a fling, the next minute we're friends and now you're talking about us finding a way forward.'

'It's what happens when two people meet, feel attracted to each other, sleep together and become friends. It's called a relationship. Friggin' hell, I'm not asking you for marriage, or to uproot your entire life, I'm asking you to give us a shot!'

'But I'm not important. I'm nothing. A fling. That's what you told your dad. I heard you.'

Ross stared at her. 'That's what this is about?' he barked out a laugh. 'Hell, Ally, I haven't had a proper conversation with my dad in ten years and I wasn't about to spill my soul to him about a girl I'm crazy about. Not within ten minutes of him saying sorry. We've got a long way to go before he becomes my best bud.'

Ally walked over to the huge windows and looked across the ocean. She so wanted to take a chance, to let Ross in, to plot a way forward to make this—whatever *this* was—work. But she knew that the further she ventured down this path the more it would hurt when the road ended at the end of a cliff.

'You really don't want to do this, do you?' Ross asked from somewhere behind her.

It wasn't that she didn't want to. It was just that she was so damn scared. What if she let him in and he let her down? What if he died? What if he met someone else and decided that person—happy, bubbly, normal—was the love of his life and she was left out in the cold?

Again.

She didn't think she could survive being left on her own again.

'Give us a shot, Ally. We're smart people, we can make this work.'

Ally heard the plea in Ross's voice, heard a hint of desperation and, worse, a smidgeon of doubt. He wasn't a hundred per cent convinced they could do that, and if he had some doubts and she a shed-load of them then what chance did they have?

Zero? Less than? And could she spend every moment waiting for the axe to fall? Maybe it was better to cut the rope holding that axe right now and get it over with.

Ally turned and looked at Ross with widened eyes filled with sorrow. 'I can't. I'm sorry.'

'Trust us—trust this,' Ross said, his eyes pleading. 'Trust me.'

Ally put her hand to her mouth and shook her head. 'I can't.'

Ross opened his mouth to say something and quickly snapped it closed. He put his hands on his hips and stared down at the table. He swore a creative streak and when he looked at her again his face was set in stone. He gestured to her laptop and the papers on her desk.

'If you need to talk to me about the campaign do it through the lawyers or through Luc. I think we're done here, Jones. You got what you wanted—a face for your campaign—and I got my heart stomped on. You probably think that's a fair trade.'

She couldn't leave it like this...couldn't let him walk out through the door feeling like this. 'Ross?'

'What?' Ross snapped, whirling around. 'What else is there to say, Ally? I love you, but you are so damn scared to take a risk on me—on us—that you would rather bury yourself in work than be with me. You are so far up your own ass that you can't even think out of the box and consider how we might make it work.'

'It's not that...' It *was* that. Of course it was that. Despite her backing off, her heart had split right in two and splattered all over the floor.

'Then what is it, huh?' Ross demanded. He stared at her, his eyes hot and hurt, and when she didn't answer the heat faded and resignation slid over his face. 'You don't love me...you don't feel the same. This was just a fling to you. I was falling in love with you and you weren't. How the hell could I have read it so wrong?'

Dear God, she loved him so much...that was the problem. She just couldn't trust... Tears rolled down her face as she struggled to find something to say...

Don't go. Don't leave me. I'm so scared...

The words were there but she couldn't spit them out. For the second time in her life her vocal cords were frozen, her tongue refused to work and her heart writhed on the floor.

Ross turned, yanked on the handle to the front door and disappeared through it. Ally's heart sent her feet a message to move but her brain kept them glued to the floor. It was better this way, the grey matter insisted. It would hurt for a while but it could be so much worse.

Ally, who couldn't catch her breath from the sobs trying to claw their way out of her throat, didn't see how.

CHAPTER TWELVE

ALLY WALKED NEXT to the pilot of the Bellechier Gulfstream jet and felt his brief touch on her back as he escorted her up the stairs into the luxurious cabin. She would never normally ask to use the jet and she fully intended to pay—*eek!*—for the privilege. But she'd pay the enormous costs just to get her sorry self out of the country, to stop her from running down the road and throwing her arms around Ross's knees and begging him to…what?

Love her? Hold her? Take her heart?

Because that was exactly what she wanted to do but she was so damn scared. If she stayed in Cape Town she would run to him. So last night, in between her sobs, she'd called Sabine and asked for the jet to collect her. Sabine, bless her, had agreed immediately and said nothing more.

Ally dumped her bag on one of the cream-coloured leather seats and rubbed her hands across her face.

'We'll be leaving in about ten minutes, Miss Jones.'

'Thanks, Paul.' Ally turned as the door to the bathroom opened and her jaw dropped as Sabine, dressed in designer jeans and a silk top, stepped out.

'Sabine, what are you doing here?' Ally asked, her eyes welling as she hurried to her and stepped into her open arms. She buried her face in Sabine's sweet-smelling neck and felt the tears build again.

'When my daughter calls in the middle of the night with a broken heart and asks to be collected I come too.' Sabine brushed Ally's hair off her face. 'Oh, baby girl, what happened?'

'It's a long story.'

Ally managed to get the words out as Sabine pulled her to a seat, sat her down and pulled the seatbelt across her lap. Settling herself in the chair next to Ally, she clicked her own belt shut and turned in her seat, holding Ally's hand in hers.

'The best stories always are,' Sabine replied as the engines rumbled below them.

Ally was dimly aware of the plane taxiing towards the runway but her head was on Sabine's shoulder and she felt… *safe*.

Her mum was here and she felt safe. Sabine wasn't her birth mother but, unlike her real mother, who'd never given a damn, she'd commandeered the plane in the middle of a cold Swiss night, dropped everything and come for her.

Ally was stunned at this demonstration of her love, but habit had her protesting.

'You didn't have to come for me. I'm fine,' Ally whispered. She lifted her head and wiped her eyes with the tips of her fingers. Then a tissue appeared, as if by magic, between Sabine's fingers and Ally grabbed it gratefully.

'You just don't get it, do you?' Sabine shook her head, her eyes deep and dark with love.

'Get what?' Ally asked, confused.

'How much I love you.'

Ally closed her eyes. 'But how could you? You're not my mother.'

'What did you say to me?' Sabine asked in French.

Oh, crap. She recognised that tone. All her kids knew that when Sabine switched to French midconversation it was a massive clue that she was at the end of her patience.

'I was your mother from the day you slid your hand into mine in that hotel room in Phuket. Who sat with you night after night in hospital as you struggled with pneumonia? Who dressed you and fed you and did hours of brain-numbing homework with you? How *dare* you utter those words to me?'

Ally wanted cover her head with her arms. 'Sabine—'

'I'm not finished. Even before your dad died who took you to school and kissed your grazes better? Bought you your first puppy and Barbie and iPod? I explained the birds and the bees to you and I kept your father and brothers off your back when you went on dates with loser boys.'

Oh, if love was action then Sabine had always showed her how much she loved her. Ally tried to speak, to apologise, but Sabine didn't give her a gap to jump in.

'Who took you to your first spa treatment, made you extra-chocolatey ice cream sundaes, picked you and your friends up from a party at three in the morning and told your father that you were home by eleven? Who wouldn't go back to work because she thought it was more important to raise you? It was *me*, you ungrateful brat! And what have you given me in return?'

'I've worked hard… I've tried to do well!' Ally said in a little voice. 'I wanted to show you how grateful I am.'

Sabine slumped back in her chair. 'I never wanted your *gratitude*, Alyssa. I wanted you. I wanted you to talk to me, to let me in, to share your soul. I wanted to be your mama, to be there for you.' Sabine sent her a piercing look. 'I wanted—I *want* to be allowed to love you. And, by the way, if you are hurting nothing will stop me from running to you, and if someone has hurt you then I will hunt them down and kill them.' Sabine thought for a moment. 'Or at least hire someone to do it.'

Ally hiccupped a small laugh. Sabine—no, her mum— would be relentless in her pursuit of revenge. 'I'm sorry. I'm so, so sorry.'

'Pfft.' And in the blink of an eye, her anger was replaced with concern. 'So who has hurt you, baby? Ross?'

Ally shook her head, twisted her fingers back into her mum's smaller hand and put her head on her shoulder. 'I did. I hurt myself. I am my own worst enemy.'

Sabine stroked her head. 'Tell me.'

Who else could she talk to about this? Nobody. Who else did she want to talk to about this? Nobody. It was time to let her in.

'We have a connection…a big one,' Ally admitted. 'I'm in love with him and I think that he might be in love with me.'

Ally didn't see Sabine's very satisfied smile. 'That's a good start.'

Ally looked past Sabine's shoulder and out of the window and dimly realised that they were in the air. She hadn't even realised that they had taken off.

'It's crazy—we haven't known each other that long and he's talking about trying to keep this…this thing going.'

'Good for him. How?'

Ally sat up, undid her seatbelt and sat cross-legged in the big chair. 'I don't know. I didn't let him get that far. I said that everything I love is in Geneva and that I can't sacrifice my career for him.'

'L'imbecile…' Sabine murmured, but gently.

'I know.' Ally looked down at her hands. 'I'm scared. I've been scared for a long, long time.'

'Of what?'

Could she say this? Did she dare?

'Of being left alone. Of experiencing love and losing it. Of not being wanted. But mostly of being left alone. It terrifies me, but—'

'But?'

'But I'm almost more afraid of not being with him than I am of being alone' Ally admitted. 'And I'm so ashamed that I've left him thinking that I don't love him.'

'You did that?'

'Mmm.'

'Then I repeat: you're an idiot,' Sabine said on a loving smile. 'Do you want me to get the plane turned around?'

Ally looked at her in shock. 'What? Why?'

'Oh, I don't know…so that you can go back and tell him the truth?'

She might be tired of being scared but she wasn't that brave. She needed to take some time to think this through…

'It would be too easy, and I don't know if he'd believe me,' Ally said quietly. 'I think I need a little time.'

'To do what?'

Ally half smiled, although her heart still felt as if it was breaking. 'To learn how to be a better daughter, friend, lover. I need to be a better listener, to gain control of my fear. I need time, Maman.'

It was the first time she'd called Sabine by that name and she liked the sound of it on her lips. Judging by Sabine's wobbly lower lip, she did too.

'You risk losing him if you take too much time, *ma petite.*'

Ally nodded. 'I know. But I won't go back to him as half a person, living in fear. If I go back—*when* I go back—it'll be because I'm strong enough to be his lover. He doesn't deserve anything less.'

Sabine didn't say anything for a long time. 'I'm so proud of you.'

'Thanks.' Ally slumped back in her chair. 'Now can you take the pain away?'

Sabine raised one shoulder in that very Gallic way. 'The pain is the proof that you can love. Own it—be proud of it.'

'It sucks,' she muttered inelegantly.

Ally stood behind her family in the media room on the Bellechier estate and held her breath as Luc inserted a CD into the system so that they could watch the final cuts for the four Bellechier commercials. Her heart was firmly in her throat.

Ross jumped out of the screen, his eyes inviting the viewers to step into his world.

The camera loved Ross and had captured his innate charisma and his love of life. Norm had done a great job, incorporating the craziness and funkiness of the open offices of RBM, and they'd all agreed to call the new Bellechier line Win!. Whether he was standing on the top of Table

Mountain at sunset or flinging his Ducati around the tight corners of Chapman's Peak Drive, every frame made you want to live his life, be part of his life, wear his clothes… be just like him.

Or, if you were female, be with him.

Mission accomplished, Ally thought, shoving her fist into that space just beneath her ribs. Her heartburn was back—an ailment she hadn't experienced in Cape Town. Probably because after a hard day's work she'd destressed by having Ross's hands on her body, his mouth on hers, him taking her every which way to Sunday.

She'd been back in Geneva for a week and she felt as if she was walking around with half of her brain and all of her heart in Cape Town. Ally pulled her bottom lip with her thumb and forefinger as the still photographs of Ross flashed up on the screen. There was the one of him sitting on the couch in his office, half smiling up at her as he told her to trust the people around her.

She'd taken that image, had it printed, and it was sitting on her bedside table. She'd spent many, many hours not sleeping and looking at him…

She didn't want to look at his photograph for the rest of her life when she could be looking at the real thing. She didn't want to struggle to remember what his hands felt like on her skin. She wanted to feel, experience, live.

Dear God, she wanted to live…with *him*.

Ross's face faded from the massive TV screen and Ally didn't hear the conversation around her—didn't take in the effusive praise, barely felt the kisses on her cheek, the arms around her shoulder squeezing her.

'I'm resigning,' she said quietly, and then with more force, 'I've got to leave.'

Luc turned around as the conversation tapered off and folded his arms across his broad chest. 'What did you say?'

Ally threw up her hands. 'I'm sorry. I'm so sorry…and after all you've done for me! I'm so grateful for the job, and the responsibility of being Brand and Image Director, but I can't any more.' She placed her hands on her face. 'I know it's ungrateful, and it's terrible timing, and that you'll hate me for it, but I need to go back to Cape Town. I need to be there.'

Ally felt Luc step forward, inhaled his cologne and allowed him to peel her fingers off her face. As always, his expression was kind and understanding.

Ally opened her mouth to talk again but Luc shook his head. 'Shut up, kid.'

Ally blinked away tears as Luc looked at his father and Patric. 'You two owe me a hundred each. She didn't last two weeks.'

As Justin and Patric reached into their wallets and looked for cash Luc's words started to make sense. 'You *bet* on me?'

'Sure.' Patric ruffled her hair after he'd handed his cash to Luc.

'Shame on you!' Sabine chastised them, sliding her hand around Ally's waist. 'Peegs!'

Justin grinned. 'Oh, you're not innocent either, my angel. We had a side bet going too.'

Ally narrowed her eyes at her mother. *'Et tu...?'*

Sabine shrugged, and then grinned. 'We all knew that you would go back to Cape Town if you could just stop being so stubborn and admit that you wanted more than just your career.'

Luc shoved the cash into his wallet as Ally rubbed the back of her neck, conscious that she now had knots on her knots. 'About my job...'

Luc shrugged. 'There's no reason why you can't work from Cape Town—maybe spending a week here every six weeks or so. Ally, you have some very well-paid, well-educated and talented people in your team and it's about time that they earned the huge salaries we're paying them. Create the vision, create the direction and then let them get on with it. Pick the projects you want to get involved in or not. Direct, delegate, advise.' Luc grinned. 'What do you think I do all day?'

'Mess about online and chat to your bimbos,' Patric grumbled. 'I would like to point out that I am the only one who, as the designer, actually does any work in this place.'

Ally flashed him a smile. 'But you are the heart of Bellechier, Patric.'

'I *so* am.'

Luc rolled his eyes at Ally. 'So, are you staying or going?'

It didn't take Ally more than a millisecond to make up her mind. She loved her job, and she'd need something to do in Cape Town or she'd drive Ross to drink. 'Staying at Bellechier. Going to Cape Town.'

'And I presume you'd like the plane?' Luc said.

Ally flashed her dimples at him. 'Yes, please.'

Luc wrapped his arm around her neck and hauled her into his chest. 'Go get him, Pork Chop.'

'He might not want me anymore,' Ally muttered into his collarbone.

'Then he'd be an idiot, and I've very good reports that he is anything but.' Luc pulled back to look down into her face. 'But if he hurts you he'll have your brothers rearranging his face.'

'And me,' Justin added.

Ally sent them a watery smile as she reached out and took Sabine's hand. 'Thanks, but he should be more scared of Maman.'

'Damn right,' Sabine agreed. 'Nobody messes with my girl.'

Ross slouched into the chair on his fully dark veranda and propped his bare feet up onto the corner of the long wooden table. When he couldn't sleep—which was all the time—he'd taken to sitting here in this chair and staring into the dark. Above him the stars in the southern hemisphere sky were partially obscured by light cloud and below him the waves used the beach as a punch bag.

He closed his eyes, saw Ally in every shadow in his mind and quickly opened them again. Frickin' hell, he simply couldn't get her out of his head. She was there in the early morning as he tried to run off his frustration and his sadness on the beach; he found himself reaching for his mobile to see if she'd sent him an e-mail or a text during meetings; she was there when he finally crawled into bed at night.

He'd tried so hard to stop loving her, to stop thinking about her, but everywhere he went she was on his mind. He so badly wanted her to fade from his memory but just as badly he wanted to recollect every minute he'd spent with her.

He'd become the basket case he'd accused her of being. Ross rubbed his jaw, hearing the rasp of his beard. He couldn't remember when last he'd shaved, when last he'd eaten something he'd actually tasted, and when he did manage to doze off his dreams all starred Ally. He couldn't decide if he hated or loved them.

A million thoughts scurried in and out of his brain but a few were lodged front and centre. They'd been so damn close to finding something special, to clicking in the way that poets and songwriters wrote of. So damn close… Had he said enough? Had he reacted too early? Had he forced her into a corner and boxed her in?

Each question twisted the long, cold spear lodged in his heart. He'd still had so much to say to her but instead he'd just watched her walk away.

Then again, he'd asked her if she loved him and she hadn't had an answer. And even *he* knew, stupid as he was when it came to women, that her non-answer meant that she didn't. And he'd have to have had the IQ of a fence pole to forget that she'd warned him that she didn't do messy emotions or attachments. Why the frig hadn't he listened?

And under the desperation, the ache for her, he was constantly, chronically angry. They could have had, could have *been*, something special. When she forgot to be closed off and walled up she was funny and sensitive and so damn sexy it took his breath away. And she adored his dog…

'Arf!' Pic barked, as if he knew exactly what Ross was thinking.

'Yeah, yeah—she loved you far more than she loved me. No need to rub it in.'

Pic gave him a look that suggested he grow a pair and stop whining. It wasn't a bad idea, Ross thought, but he rather liked wallowing—especially when there was no one to witness it except for Pic. And who was *he* going to tell?

'Arf, arf, arf!' Pic bark-shouted again, his tone suggesting that Ross should not test his powers.

'I'm talking to a damned dog,' he murmured, rolling his head to try and ease the tension that had become his favourite companion—not counting the four-legged sarcasm machine at his feet.

So tomorrow he'd get up, get dressed, go to work, he thought. Just as he'd done every day since she'd left. Maybe tomorrow he'd recapture the joy he felt in his work; hopefully he wouldn't spend another day just going through the motions.

Maybe he'd call up a few mates, have them round for a barbecue, surf later and throw back a few beers, pretend everything was back to normal.

Or maybe—and this was far more likely—he'd sit here again tomorrow night, alone and miserable, with a whisky bottle close to his elbow and an empty, throbbing soul.

CHAPTER THIRTEEN

ROSS CAUGHT A wave to the beach, stepped off his board into the shallows and wished that he could just go back in and stay there. When he was flying down the waves he temporarily forgot that he was bloody miserable and…and lonely, dammit.

He tucked his board under his arm and shoved his hair back off his face. He had little reason to feel so…so *flat*, he thought. Yeah, he'd lost a girl, but his life was still full. He was financially fluid, his relationship with his family was better than ever, he had lots of friends and a roaring business. If he needed a woman he could do it the old-fashioned way: head down to a pub and pick someone up.

The thought made him want to throw up. Not only had Jones taken his heart, it seemed she'd also taken his sex drive too. Just another aspect of this very crappy situation.

Ross whistled for Pic and frowned when he saw that he wasn't where he'd left him, lying next to the huge piece of driftwood where he and Ally had always sat when they came down to the beach. Ross felt his heart lurch in panic. Pic—so well trained—would never have left his spot unless there'd been a problem. Had he been dognapped? He'd lost his woman—losing his dog would put him right over the edge.

Desperately trying to keep calm, Ross whistled again and finally heard that answering familiar bark. He whirled around, surfboard wobbling, and there was Pic, his long ears bouncing as he ran.

Ross would later swear he had the biggest smile on his face.

'Arf-arf-arf-arf-arf!'

Ross bent down as Pic reached him, quickly running his hands over his body to check if he was injured, looking for a clue as to why he'd leave his spot. 'Why d'ya leave, Picky? Why, huh?'

'Arf-arf-arf-arf-arf!' Pic shouted back, then twisted around and bolted down the beach.

Ross shouted at him to return, but instead he ran full-tilt at the waves to a slim figure who stood in the shallows, a stick in her hand. Ross watched as she lifted the stick and threw it into the water. Pic plunged into the waves after it.

Ally.

Ross dropped his board, put his hands on his thighs and hoped that his heart wasn't about to jump out of his ribcage. She was dressed as casually as he'd ever seen in her, in cotton shorts that stopped midthigh and a tight-fitting crop top that showed off a strip of her belly. Her hair was tucked under a baseball cap and big shades covered her eyes. If it wasn't for Pic then he might not even have noticed her standing on the beach, the sea playing amongst her bare toes.

This is it, Ally thought, looking sideways.

She could feel Ross's hard eyes on her, yet he didn't come any closer, didn't make a move. Ally sighed. Could she blame him? She was the one who'd walked, who'd left him with words of love on his lips… Why should he do a damn thing?

No, she owed it to him to make the first move, she thought as Pic dropped the stick at her feet, lay down on his tummy and looked up at her with his I'll-die-if-you-don't eyes. She smiled, picked up the stick and tossed it again. When he'd bounded off she made her way through the shallows to where Ross was standing, his expression forbidding.

'Hi,' she said quietly, wishing she could touch him. His hand, his arm, his face…anywhere.

'I should've guessed you were back when I couldn't find

my damn dog. Pic wouldn't leave his spot for anyone but you,' Ross said in a rough voice.

'He looked so sad, waiting for you, that I thought I'd play with him for a bit,' Ally said, her words spilling out in a heated rush.

Ross picked his board up, pushed it nose down into the sand and folded his arms across his bare chest. 'What are you doing here, Alyssa?'

Ally twisted her fingers together. 'That's a good question…'

'Does it have an answer? Maybe some time this century?'

Ally winced at the ice in his tone. Pic bounded up to them again, the stick in his mouth. Ross grabbed him before its pointed ends could scrape either of them, commanded Pic to drop the stick and stay.

Pic dropped the stick and stayed, but not before humphing out an unamused bark and turning his back on Ross. Ally bit her lip to keep from smiling at Ross's fur person.

'He's been impossible since you left,' Ross muttered. 'You spoilt him.'

'And you spoilt me,' Ally said. 'And I've been impossible since I left too.'

Ross waited a beat before responding. 'You are always bloody impossible, so how was it different this time?' he said in a weary voice.

Ally gestured to their spot by the driftwood and felt relieved when Ross walked over to the log, rested his butt against the hard wood and crossed his legs at the ankles. Water sat in fat beads on his skin and rolled off his hair. As per usual he hadn't brought a towel with him to the beach, preferring to jump into the shower after surfing. Preferably with her.

But if she had to judge by his inscrutable face a repeat of that wasn't likely.

Ross sighed, clenched the hand that rested on his thick thigh and lifted one eyebrow. 'I'm not going to stand here and play guessing games with you. Say what you want to say and let's get this done.'

He wasn't going to make this easy for her and she couldn't blame him. 'I'm sorry I walked away.'

'You flew six thousand miles to tell me that?'

'Yes…no… That was part of it.' Ally pulled off her cap and glasses and tossed them to the sand. Her hair tumbled down and a couple of strands caught the evening breeze and danced around her face. She held them back with one hand. 'You hinted that you might love me.'

'It wasn't a bloody hint. I came right out and said it,' Ross retorted, obviously unhappy with the idea.

'Do you still? Love me?'

'Unfortunately it's not an emotion I can switch on and off, despite some major effort on my part,' Ross snarled. 'Is there a point to this? Because if you've come to rub my nose in it then you can just sod off again.'

Ally gathered what little courage she had left and forced out the words that would change her life for ever. 'I'm trying—very badly—to tell you that I feel the same.'

'So?'

Ally frowned, puzzled. 'I thought you might want to know that.'

Ross said in a deadpan voice, 'Am I supposed to drop down, put my feet in the air and wait for you to rub my stomach? You're confusing me with my dog.' Ross pushed himself up and sent her a hot glance. 'Hearing that doesn't mean a hell of a lot—especially since I know that there's nothing backing it.'

'What do you mean?' Ally cried, her heart pounding with fear. She was losing him all over again, and this time it hurt even more.

'So you love me, huh? So what? What does that mean anyway? Words are empty unless you've got the guts to back up the words with action, Jones. Got any action, sweetheart?'

Ross looked at her for a long time and when she didn't speak again sent her a look full of disappointment.

'Didn't think so.'

He clicked his fingers and Pic stood up and sent her a longing look. At least *he* seemed sorry to leave her behind.

Ally watched his broad back walk away from her and a surge of anger pumped up from her belly and heated her veins. Without thought she hurtled across the sand and punched him in the shoulder. Ross took a half-step forward before spinning around.

'What the hell, Jones…?'

Ally felt the heat in her face, down her throat, mottling her throat. For good measure she let her fist fly into his shoulder again, just to make damn sure he was paying attention. 'You want action? You want proof that I love you?'

'It would be nice,' Ross replied, rubbing the spot where she'd punched him. 'And don't hit me again!'

'Proof? Well, okay, then. Does packing up my stuff and renting out my apartment count?'

Ross's eyes half closed and his entire body went on alert. 'It depends where that luggage is heading.'

'It's in storage at the moment, waiting for me to tell them where to send it,' Ally retorted. 'Okay, let's try something else out and see how it fits your definition of—' she made air quotes with her fingers '—*action*. I tried to resign from Bellechier so that I could come back here to you.'

'And they didn't accept your resignation, so you're stuck with the job you love above everything else?' Ross twisted his lips and lifted up his hand, looking suddenly weary. 'Look, Ally, until you are actually ready to tell me that you're coming back here for good, let's just table this conversation, okay?'

'I'm ready to come back here for good.'

Ross blinked and blinked again, looking confused and adorable. He ran his hand across his jaw. 'That's not funny, Al.'

'I'm not joking. And if you gave me a minute to explain,

instead of just jumping to conclusions, then we could stop talking and start kissing—and I *really* want to get to the kissing part.'

Humour, relief, anticipation finally sparked in his eyes, so Ally let out the breath she was holding and took his right hand in both of hers.

'Sorry, I just need to touch you.'

Ross bent his knees so that he could look directly into her eyes. 'Explain, sweetheart, *please*. You're taking years off my life here.'

'Tu es beau. Tu me fascines. Je veux être avec toi pour toujours. Tu es l'amour de ma vie. Ma chérie tu me fais très heureux.'

'Not any clearer…'

'It's funny that I can find exactly what I want to say in French, but in English not so much.' Ally blew out a breath, frustrated with herself. 'All these phrases are running around my head and I can't adequately translate them. They don't work in English.'

'Well, you're going to have to try, sweetheart, before I explode from frustration.'

Ally sucked in her cheeks and lifted emotion-saturated eyes. 'You are beautiful,' she whispered softly. 'I'm passionate about you. I want to be with you for ever. You are the love of my life. You fascinate me… Not necessarily in that order.'

Ross placed his forehead against hers. 'Yeah…that'll work.'

'Je t'aime, Ross.'

'That one I don't need a translation for. *Je t'aime* back, sweetheart.'

Ally smiled through her tears. 'As I said, I tried to hand in my resignation but Luc wouldn't accept it. He felt that I could work from here and spend a week in Geneva every six weeks or so. I'd need an office, a high-speed internet connection, a laptop…'

Ross straightened and rested his other hand on her hip. 'Done, done and done.'

'And I need *you*. I don't care about the job if I have you.' Ally wrinkled her nose. 'Well, I do a little bit—'

Ross chuckled. 'A little bit?'

'Okay, a lot. But not if it means being alone, being without you,' Ally said, staring at her smaller hand in his.

Then she started to spill her soul.

'I don't want to work fourteen-hour days and go home to an empty apartment. I want to work six-hour days and play with your dog while you surf. I want to learn to cook so that we can drink wine in the kitchen together as we make our meals. I want to listen to you tell me about your day and your crazy staff and I want to do the same. I want to walk upstairs with you at night, make delicious love with you and fall asleep to the sound of your heart thumping beneath my ear. I want to love you. I want to be loved by you.'

Ross pulled her into him. 'You've got it, darling. All of that and more.'

He stared down into her face for a long time, still drinking her in.

'I can't believe you are here.' He held her narrow face in his large hands and ran his thumbs across her bottom lip.

'Is this when the kissing starts?' Ally demanded, laughing at him.

'This is when everything starts, my darling,' Ross replied, his heart thumping. 'You…me…our lives. I love you.'

Ally sighed, closing her eyes in pleasure at his words. 'I love you. I've never said that to anyone before.'

'Well, I like it that I'm the first man you've said it to, but I intend to be the last man you say it to.'

Ally shook her head. 'No… I mean, you don't understand. My dad never told me he loved me andy while the Bellechiers say it with impunity, I've never been able to say those words. I was always too…scared.'

Ross's arms held her firm against his chest. 'Don't ever be afraid to say them—to me or to them. It's a pretty powerful phrase.'

Ally listened to his heartbeat, content to stand on the light, bright, sunny beach. 'How did it go with your dad? I wanted to ask you, but—'

Ross tipped her head up with a finger under her chin. 'We'll talk later… I think it's high time the kissing began.'

Ross started at the corner of her mouth and felt the tilt of her lips as she smiled, felt the last little eddies of tension swirl away as his hands ran over her shoulders, down her arms, up her sides. Holding her ribcage with both hands, he spread his fingers so that his thumbs brushed her nipples and they immediately flowered under his attention. Her tongue met his in a long, lust-soaked tangle and he went from hard to concrete in a nanosecond.

She was back in his arms, in his life, for good, for ever, and it felt more than right.

It felt like perfection.

'Let's go back to your place,' she suggested, desperate to get her hands on him.

Ross shook his head and lifted her chin so that she looked directly into his love-soaked, passionate eyes.

'From now on there is no your place or my place; we're in this together. It's all ours, sweetheart. You and me…'

'And Pic,' Ally added quickly, her hand on his head.

'And Pic.'

Ross jogged down the beach, picked up his surfboard, and when he returned slung his arm around her shoulder and guided her home.

'About Pic… Can you please talk to him about drinking out of the toilet bowl? It's his latest trick and it's gross. He listens to you.'

'Pic, don't drink out of the toilet bowl,' Ally told his—their—dog, her smile wide.

'Arf!' Pic barked his agreement and two seconds later, let out a volley of barks again.

Ally placed her hand on his head and sent Ross a naughty grin. 'And yes, Pic, of course you can keep on chewing on his flip flops.'

* * * * *

A sneaky peek at next month...

MODERN tempted™

TRUE LOVE AND TEMPTATION!

My wish list for next month's titles...

In stores from 20th June 2014:

❏ Her Hottest Summer Yet – Ally Blake

❏ Who's Afraid of the Big Bad Boss?

  – Nina Harrington

In stores from 4th July 2014:

❏ If Only... – Tanya Wright

❏ Only the Brave Try Ballet – Stefanie London

Available at WHSmith, Tesco, Asda, Eason, Amazon and Apple

Just can't wait?

Visit us Online

You can buy our books online a month before they hit the shops! **www.millsandboon.co.uk**

0614/31

Special Offers

Every month we put together collections and longer reads written by your favourite authors.

Here are some of next month's highlights— and don't miss our fabulous discount online!

On sale 20th June   On sale 4th July   On sale 4th July

Save 20%
on all Special Releases

THE
CHATSFIELD®

Collect all 8!

Buy now at
www.millsandboon.co.uk/thechatsfield

THE
CHATSFIELD®

Enter the intriguing online world of
The Chatsfield and discover secret
stories behind closed doors…

www.thechatsfield.com

Check in online now for your exclusive
welcome pack!

Discover more romance at

www.millsandboon.co.uk

- ❤ WIN great prizes in our exclusive competitions
- ❤ BUY new titles before they hit the shops
- ❤ BROWSE new books and REVIEW your favourites
- ❤ SAVE on new books with the Mills & Boon® Bookclub™
- ❤ DISCOVER new authors

PLUS, to chat about your favourite reads, get the latest news and find special offers:

- 🇫 Find us on facebook.com/millsandboon
- 🐦 Follow us on twitter.com/millsandboonuk
- ❤ Sign up to our newsletter at millsandboon.co.uk